"I struggle every damn day not knowing what to do, how to handle things for them. Worrying I'll do something wrong and screw them up forever."

"Just keep loving them as you are." She started to pull away, but he touched her cheek, held her in place.

"You're one hell of a woman, Mackenzie Campbell. I'm really glad you came to our ranch."

He drew back and she couldn't look away. Pain, relief, maybe even desire flickered across his face.

Closing the distance, keeping his eyes on hers, he finally touched his lips to hers. His mouth slid across hers in a joining so sweet she ached. His fingers slid down her cheek to her neck, and she wondered if he could feel her pulse galloping, wild and free.

He stilled, just for a moment, and just as she started to pull back, he slanted his mouth over hers and took the kiss deep. So deep she didn't think—no, she knew she'd never been kissed that way before.

Dear Reader,

Welcome to the third book in my Cowboys to Grooms series! Thank you for coming back to read Hunter's story, and to see who he falls head over heels in love with. Hunter is a charmer, a flirt and a dedicated dad to his adorable triplet sons. Mackenzie is a stuntwoman from Scotland, and she has literally tumbled into Hunter's heart. I had so much fun writing about her and coming up with the stories she tells Cody, Tripp and Eli. (And it's made me want to go to Scotland even more now!) Mackenzie is the first woman who can see past his flirting to what matters the most to Hunter—he's definitely met his match in her.

All the characters in my Cowboys to Grooms series have become so alive to me over the course of the last two years. I've laughed, cried and had a wonderful time writing each of these books, and I hope you're enjoying spending time with Nash, Wyatt, Hunter, Kade and Luke.

I hope to finish out the series with Kade's and Luke's stories in the near future. Please visit me at allisonbcollins.com for updates. I'd love to hear from you! Drop me a line at allisonbcollins@outlook.com and let me know what you think of Hunter and Mackenzie's story.

Thank you, and happy reading!

Allison

HOME *on the* RANCH

THE MONTANA COWBOY'S TRIPLETS

⚒

ALLISON B. COLLINS

HARLEQUIN® HOME ON THE RANCH

Recycling programs
for this product may
not exist in your area.

ISBN-13: 978-1-335-47489-6

Home on the Ranch: The Montana Cowboy's Triplets

Copyright © 2019 by Allison B. Collins

Printed in U.S.A.

Allison B. Collins is an award-winning author and a fifth-generation Texan, so it's natural for her to love all things Western. It's a tough job to spend evenings writing about cowboys, rodeos and precocious children, but Allison is willing to do it to bring them all to life. She lives in Dallas with her hero husband of thirty years, who takes great care of her and their four rambunctious cats.

Books by Allison B. Collins

Harlequin Western Romance

Cowboys to Grooms

A Family for the Rancher
Falling for the Rebel Cowboy

Visit the Author Profile page
at Harlequin.com for more titles.

To Mother.

I hope heaven has bookstores
so you can keep reading my books.

Acknowledgments

First and foremost, thank you to my husband
of thirty years. You're the best man I know,
and I'm so glad I said YES! Thanks for
always taking care of me, and encouraging me
to go on this journey to publication.

I have the best friends and critique partners
in the world. Thank you Angela Hicks,
Sasha Summers and Suzanne Clark
for reading and loving my Sullivan brothers!
I truly can't do this without you all.

To Johanna Raisanen, editor extraordinaire.
Thank you for believing in me and my cowboys.
I love working with you and Harlequin Books!

A deep thanks to all my friends who read my books
and give me encouragement every single day.
I love you all!

Chapter 1

Hunter Sullivan inhaled air so crisp and cold he could swear icicles were forming inside his nose. He raised the collar of his jacket, wishing now he'd worn a heavier coat. Might have been late March, but around here, folks still considered it winter. Clouds hung low over the snow-covered Montana mountains, and a layer of frost covered the valley floor like an ice-skating rink.

Reining Becket to a stop on top of the small plateau, he looked out over the valley he loved. He and his older brothers had grown up here, running roughshod and free, and he couldn't imagine living anywhere else. Forget cities, big or small. This was where he belonged, living and working on the family guest ranch. The buildings and cabins spread throughout the valley, surrounded by mountains and towering trees. Some days the lake was so still it mirrored the surrounding landscape and sky.

Heaven on earth.

Well, heaven until a few days ago, when a caravan of trucks and trailers and Tinseltown trespassers invaded their ranch.

Becket snorted and stamped his hooves, ready to gallop across frozen fields. "Okay, bud, I know you want to run." Hunter patted Becket's neck.

His horse whinnied, and Hunter glanced over his shoulder just as two of his brothers joined him on the rise.

Hunter shot a look at Wyatt. "Why aren't you at home with your bride?"

"Frankie's on a video call with her dad's office. You shoulda seen her—face made up, wearing a silk blouse on top, Scooby Doo pajama bottoms and SpongeBob slippers."

"Dude, SpongeBob? Were they a wedding gift from you?" Luke teased.

"Johnny picked them out for her. When you take a four-year-old shopping, you get the cool clothes." Wyatt gave a sheepish grin, but parental pride colored the words.

"You're technically still honeymooners, right? You should go home and coax her out of the pj's." Hunter jerked his thumb back toward the family cabins.

"I would, but I gotta head out to the south fence and fix the gate."

"Dad was right to make you foreman." Luke rested his hands on the pommel and rocked back.

Wyatt did a double take. "Where'd that come from?"

"Just sayin'. You slid right in when Shorty retired, and you've kept things running great." Luke stretched his arm out and gave Wyatt a fist bump.

"Thanks," Wyatt said, a note of surprise in his voice. He'd had a lot of rough years, and rarely heard praise from anyone.

"Where you headed to?" Hunter glanced at Luke.

"I wanted a few minutes of quiet before I start making rounds. Wellness checks for the animals the movie crew brought in."

"They got you doing double duty with their livestock? Hope we're charging 'em for your vet services," Wyatt said.

"Part of the contract, and yeah, we're charging—" Movement to the left caught Hunter's eye, and he saw a black horse racing at a full gallop across the frosty valley.

But the horse wasn't on its own.

There was a woman in the saddle.

He squinted. The woman's body was tilting to the side. It looked like she was hanging on tight. At that speed, if she fell off or got thrown, she'd be seriously hurt. Maybe even killed.

"Hey. You see that?" Luke leaned forward.

"I got this." Hunter squeezed his knees against Becket's sides. "Hiyah." Becket leaped forward and stretched his neck, galloping toward the woman.

Hunter gripped the reins so tight his fingers went numb. Memories of the last runaway horse flashed through his head like a rapid-fire slideshow. His vision wavered, then tunneled, and his pulse kept time with the pounding of Becket's hooves.

He drew closer, and Hunter saw long red curls streaming behind the woman like dragon fire. *Carley?* A celebrity, Carley Williams was the lead actress filming the modern-day Western on the ranch, and in the short time he'd spent flirting with her, he'd gotten the feeling she wasn't much of a horsewoman.

"Hang on! I'm coming."

"Back off. I don't need anyone." Carley pulled herself back up into the saddle.

Becket eased up next to them and kept pace with the other horse, and Hunter reached for the reins.

She knocked his hand away.

He reached out and latched onto the reins, and it became a tug of war. What was with her? "Whoa, there, whoa. Easy." Both horses slowed to a canter, then a complete stop, and he could finally breathe again. "You okay? What spooked your horse?"

The woman punched his arm. "You blooming idiot! Why'd ye stop me? You could have died, and taken me to hell with ye!"

This wasn't the woman he'd been flirting with since the movie people arrived. She had the same hair as Carley and kinda looked like her. But the accent…and that punch… He rubbed his arm. She definitely had some muscles. "Your horse was out of control. Are you okay?"

"We weren't out of control, you bampot."

He didn't know what *bampot* meant, but he figured it wasn't *studly hero*. "Your horse was galloping at breakneck speed, and you were damn near close to breaking your own neck."

"I'm rehearsing. I know what I'm doing." Red spots of color made her cheeks glow, and her eyes flashed emerald fire.

"Rehearsing?"

She huffed, and whipped her cowboy hat off to shove her hair out of her eyes. "I'm a stunt double."

He tipped his head as her words sank in. "You're what?"

"A stuntwoman."

"So your horse wasn't out of control?"

"Are ye daft? I already said no. Rory and I have made several movies together—we know what we're doing.

We're a team." She scrubbed a hand over the horse's neck, and it seemed to preen with her attention.

"Sorry." He took his hat off, then reset it on his head. How was he to have known who she was? "But racing your horse like that is dangerous. You don't know this terrain, which puts you both at risk. I've seen what happens when a horse is out of control—you can't blame me for worrying you were in trouble." He tugged his hat lower.

"I've already ridden the valley twice. We're fine. Go on about yer business." She gathered up the reins. "Go ruin someone else's day."

"Fine. Later." This time he did gallop off, but he glanced back to see her watching him. *Stubborn, ornery female. So* not his type of woman. He really hoped he wouldn't run into her too often. He'd be sure to stay away from her in the future. He didn't date a lot, but he liked feminine flowers, not tumbleweed tomboys.

He wheeled his horse around and saw Luke and Wyatt watching him, laughing their stupid heads off. "Dammit." Hunter winced. *Might as well get it over with.*

"Did you rescue the fair maiden, bro?" Luke smirked.

"Shaddup." He knew his ears had to be red. "You were thinking the same thing. I was just faster at being the hero. Gotta get back."

He split off from them to return to the lodge and start the day. On the way to the barn, he saw the movie crew working around their set. Carley Williams sat in a director's chair with her name on it, reading a thick stack of paper. Her long red hair hung loose, but it didn't shine as much as he'd thought it had the other day.

Carley looked up and saw him. She waved, and he noticed her thin red gloves. They looked more like a fashion accessory than something that would keep her hands warm in the cold snap.

He dismounted and tied the reins to a fence post, then walked over to her. Small heaters were spaced around her chair, going full blast. Taking his hat off, he grinned at her. "Mornin'."

"Hi, Hunter. I was just thinking about you." She smiled up at him, all Scarlett O'Hara–like. It still knocked him back that a big-time celebrity had started flirting with him when she'd arrived at the ranch.

"Are you filming today?"

"I am." She held up a script. "I'm going over lines one more time."

The director, Tom something or other, joined them. "Hunter, right?"

"Yep."

"Great ranch you have here. Although you'd do well to have better cell reception. Had a helluva time getting through to the producer last night."

"Sorry, sir. That's what we get for living out here. Away from crowds, cars and congestion." Hunter watched the man's eyes constantly moving over the ranch, the set, his team, and doubted any of the sarcasm had gotten through to him.

Hoofbeats echoed across the way, and he saw the stuntwoman back from her ride. She dismounted and started to walk her horse into the barn, her long brown coat flapping around her legs.

"Mackenzie! Come on over here," the director shouted to her.

She glanced toward them, then handed the reins to someone, patted her horse's neck and started walking their way. Hunter could have sworn her steps faltered when she saw him standing with Carley and Tom.

"Yes?"

"How'd it go? Did you get the runaway horse scene blocked out?"

"Aye. There was one bloody idiotic problem, but I took care of it." She glanced again at Hunter, her eyes speaking volumes—probably curse words.

"Good, good. Hunter, have you met Mackenzie yet? She's Carley's stunt double. Mackenzie Campbell, meet Hunter Sullivan."

Hunter shook her hand, not too surprised by her firm grip. "Nice to meet you, ma'am." He tipped his hat at her.

Her eyebrows crinkled just a bit, then smoothed out. "I need to take care of Rory, if you'll excuse me."

"Mackenzie, check in with the stunt coordinator. Hunter, you're welcome to stay and watch, as long as you're out of the way." The director walked off toward a tent.

"Oh, stay, honey. You can see me in action." Carley ran her hand down his arm.

He glanced up to see Mackenzie roll her eyes and turn away, taking off her coat as she walked and shaking it out.

"Honestly, that girl is always a mess. She's such a tomboy." Carley flipped her long curls over her shoulder and batted her eyes at him.

He backed up a step. "I should let you get to work. Got things to do at the barn."

"I finish early. Maybe we can get together." She ran a fingernail down the buttons on his jacket.

Carley was beautiful and flirtatious. The perfect woman for him to spend time with—so why did her flirting leave him cold now?

She leaned up and kissed his cheek, then turned away and walked toward the director.

He went back to Becket and led him the rest of the way to the barn. As they entered, he heard a soft voice speaking a language he'd never heard. Mackenzie stood at the other end of the barn, brushing her horse down.

She glanced up at him just as he slowed his steps. Her lips compressed into a flat line, and he could almost see her fighting to keep words from escaping.

He led Becket to his stall opposite her horse and went about the unsaddling process, then grabbed a curry-comb. The last thing he needed to do was have an argument with her, so he decided to play nice. "Where are you from? Ireland?"

"Och, don't be daft. The Highlands of Scotland."

"You're a long way from home. What brought you to America?"

She shrugged but didn't pause the brushstrokes. "I followed the work."

"Where'd you learn to ride like that?"

"You mean like I'm falling off?" She continued brushing her horse, not looking up.

"Yeah."

"Horses on the farm, and brothers who one-upped each other with dares and insults."

"How many brothers?"

"Four." She walked around to the other side of Rory, and continued brushing.

"I've got four older brothers, so I guess we have something in common."

She finally looked up at him, irritation oozing from her expression. "Tom said your last name is Sullivan. As in the name on the sign over the main entrance?"

"Yeah. I'm a co-owner."

"I don't think we have much in common after all."

"What's that supposed to mean?" *Jeez, prickly much?*

"You grew up on a luxury ranch, with ranch hands, servants…"

"Hey, this is also a working cattle ranch. I've busted my butt plenty over the years."

This time she looked up at him, pausing the brush. "Touchy, aren't you?"

He reined in his impatience, vowed to ignore her and not get into a sniping match. For some reason he didn't want to give Miss Scotland the satisfaction. He glanced at his watch, realized he had to hurry up and finish.

Try to be friendly to someone and they bite your head off. He'd have to be careful around the crabby stuntwoman. Plenty of people thought he and his brothers had it easy living on the guest ranch. That chapped his backside. They all worked hard to keep the place afloat. Every one of them still mucked out stalls, trained horses, rode herd on the cattle and did daily chores. Sure he had an office job now, but he helped his brothers out whenever, wherever they needed him.

Nash, his oldest brother, took care of everything horse-related. Plus he and his wife, Kelsey, had started an equine therapy program for wounded veterans, like himself.

Kade was the architect of the family. Hunter had helped out building new cabins on the property plenty of times, including the recent expansion of his own home. Nothing like pounding nails to get the frustrations out.

Wyatt had returned to the ranch after being gone for ten years, and settled into the foreman position. He had a new wife and cute stepson, so Hunter had taken on some additional chores to give him time with his family.

Luke was the veterinarian, not just for their ranch, but several surrounding ranches, so he always needed extra help. Hunter had helped birth cows, horses, sheep and goats, as well as cats and dogs.

The fact that this stuntwoman thought he was rich and lazy really pissed him off. He brushed Becket's coat till it gleamed under the lights of the barn, mucked out the stall, then got the horse settled with a bucket of feed. Hunter walked toward the door to leave.

"You mentioned a runaway horse earlier. It wasna' yours, was it?"

His hand stilled on the door. He'd tried for years to stuff the memories into a lockbox in his head. But every so often, he'd see something—even a little something— and the terror on the ranch hand's face would claw its way out of that lockbox and into his mind.

Hunter had only been a kid that horrible day. He knew he couldn't have helped Jed, but his heart still hurt for the guy. A mountain lion had spooked Jed's horse, slashed at its hindquarters and it had taken off, racing across the valley. Jed tried to hold on, but he kept slipping, slipping, slipping, until he'd fallen off the horse. Now he got around in a wheelchair instead of on a stallion.

"No, it wasn't me. But I saw it."

He glanced up, watched her brushing Rory, her hand moving methodically, up and down, up and down.

"I'm sorry I scared you today." Her head turned sideways, but she didn't meet his eyes, then she gave Rory her attention again.

He concentrated on stuffing the visions away again, swallowed against his tight throat.

The barn door creaked as he left the building and walked into the cold wind. It cooled his cheeks, settled him once again. He brushed straw off his jeans and caught a whiff of himself. Definitely needed a shower before heading to the office. He turned back once, and a flash of red caught his attention. Mackenzie stood in the open doorway, her eyes on him.

She touched the tip of her finger to her hat in acknowledgment, then walked up the path to the lodge.

She was fractious as a wild mustang, and she'd be harder to handle than a riled-up porcupine, but damned if he didn't have the urge to follow her up the trail.

Chapter 2

The next morning, Mackenzie carried her suitcase and backpack to the front desk in the guest ranch's cavernous lobby. Comfortable furnishings in wood and rich, dark leather were scattered around, creating an inviting atmosphere.

She liked the ranch buildings and cabins she'd set eyes on so far. They'd all been designed to be a part of the landscape, not to overwhelm it. The owners catered to people with money, yes, but the ranch wasn't an over-the-top showplace, like so many in Los Angeles.

The lady who had checked her in previously stood at the big desk again this morning. "Good morning, Ms. Campbell. How may I help you?"

Mackenzie glanced at the nameplate on the desk. "Mornin', Donna. I seem to be in need of another room."

"Oh, dear. Is there a problem with the one you were assigned?"

"Not with the room itself. My roommate woke up with the flu and if I get sick, too, it'll push production off schedule." She sighed. "Do you have another room available?"

Donna checked a computer screen. "Hold on a sec. I'll be right back." She walked through a door behind her.

Across the room, the main doors banged open, letting in a burst of cold air. She turned around as whoops echoed in the rafters, and three little boys wearing cowboy hats hurled themselves into the lobby. They raced over the furniture, thundered up the steps and back down, all while pointing imaginary guns at each other and punctuating them with *pow pows* and *bang bangs*.

They split up and one of them ran straight at her. She braced herself for the impact, and he plowed into her. She let her body go fluid and fell into a backward somersault, then lay still, flat on her back. She cracked one eye open a slit to see the horrified look on the boy's face as the other two joined him.

"Is she dead?" one of them whispered.

"I dunno." The one who'd hit her sniffled.

"Well, poke her," the third boy said.

That earned him a shove. "You poke her."

"I'll do it." Number One reached a small hand toward her.

"Wait!" Number Two snatched Number One's hand. "You don't want cooties if she's dead. Get a stick."

She heard shuffling feet and cracked an eye open again to see them tripping, shoving and racing toward the big doors. Now was her chance. She got up and held her arms out in front of her, palms limp, and started moaning. Keeping her legs stiff, she walked toward them, moving like a zombie.

The boys turned around and their eyes got so big she had to bite the inside of her cheek so she wouldn't laugh.

"Lady, what's wrong with you?" the boy in the red shirt asked, backing away from her.

"I'm the ghost of Mackenzie Campbell," she moaned, thickening her accent. "I will haunt you forever for running me over." In that instant, she noticed they didn't just look like brothers—they were identical.

She kept going, and the boys backed away. The door behind them slammed open, letting in a gust of cold air. The boys screeched to a halt, ending up in a pile of tangled limbs.

Hunter walked into the lobby and looked from them to Mackenzie playing zombie. "Uh, what's going on here?"

She grinned and dropped her hands to her hips. "Well, laddies. The jig is up."

They all turned to stare at her. "Hey, you're not dead!" said the boy wearing a blue long-sleeved shirt.

"Nay, no' yet at least." A pang hit deep in her gut. It was the truth. Thoughts of the fire months ago sprang to mind. But she couldn't think about that now—not with an upcoming scene that involved another fire.

"Hey, how come you talk funny?" Red shirt squinted up at her.

"Tripp, that's not nice. Are you all bothering Miss Campbell?" Hunter walked closer.

Honestly, the man was too handsome for his own good. Every hair in place, and a boyish wave right in front. Her fingers itched to muss it up.

The boys all stared at him, and she could see them trying to decide how best to answer.

"The lads and I were playing while I wait for the front-desk lady to come back."

All three boys turned as one to stare at her, their cute, freckled faces displaying varying degrees of surprise.

Hunter cocked his head to the right and raised a perfectly shaped eyebrow. "Not sure I believe that."

"It's true, isn't it?" She looked at the boys and winked.

"Yup!" the boy in blue shouted.

"Are you playing hooky from school again?" Hunter asked.

"No, Daddy." The boy in the blue shirt hurled himself at Hunter's leg. "It's recess."

She looked from the boys to Hunter. "These are *your* hooligans?"

"Yup."

"Well, I'll be knackered." The man who'd gotten under her skin was responsible enough to have three children? "So, who is who?" She studied the boys one by one.

"I'm Cody," Blue Shirt said.

"Tripp," Red Shirt said.

The boy in the green shirt, who had plowed into her, dug the toe of his boot into the floor.

"And who might you be?" She held her hand out to him.

"Eli." He stared at her hand for a few seconds, then shook it.

"Ye're a fine bunch of young men, aren't ye now? It's a pleasure to make your acquaintance." She perched on the arm of the lounge chair and beckoned them all closer, leaning forward like a coconspirator. "If you think playing cowboys is fun, you should play Scottish warriors. If you're real good, I'll teach you how to do it."

The boys cheered and looked at her with newfound respect. Just like her younger brothers—anyone who could teach them how to misbehave would be okay in their book.

She looked up to see Hunter staring at her, his eyebrows up his forehead. "What?"

"Nothing."

The door behind the counter opened, and Donna walked back to the front desk. "Ms. Campbell, I'm so sorry. I checked with the manager, and we don't have any other rooms or cabins available at the moment."

What will I do now? She really needed this job, needed to get back to work.

"Why do you need another room?" Hunter asked.

"My roommate has the flu."

Eli looked up at Hunter. "Daddy, she can stay with us."

"Oh, no, I couldn't—"

"There must be something available, Donna."

He had such a panicked look on his face, Mackenzie almost burst out laughing. It would serve him right if she did have to stay at his home.

"Come on, Daddy. Pleeeeaaase?" Cody held his hands up as if beseeching Hunter.

"My dad has an extra room." Hunter pulled a cell phone out of his pocket. "I'll call him."

"Bunny said they started the remodel—the room is just studs now," Donna said.

"Call Kade. See if the newest cabins—"

"He reported in earlier this morning—weather delayed some materials, so construction can't be completed."

"I guess we don't have a choice." Hunter looked up at Mackenzie.

"Is there a hotel in town?" Mackenzie crossed her fingers behind her back.

"It's an hour away, or more, depending on weather.

Your director wouldn't like it. You might get stranded in town," Donna said.

There had to be another way. His kids were cute, but she didn't want to be that close to Handsome Hunter and his high-handed ways.

He rubbed the back of his neck. "We'll just make the best of it. The old part of my cabin will give you privacy."

"No, I can't."

"Yeah, you can."

"Don't you need to ask your wife before you bring a strange woman home?"

"There's no one—"

"Mommy's an angel now." The little boy named Eli looked up at her.

She looked down at the triplets, her own grief rising like an overflowing loch. "I'm sorry, boys." She knelt on the floor in front of them. "I lost my own mum and dad when I was young. I'll bet she loved you verra much, and even now is always keepin' watch over you. She's your guardian angel."

Eli sniffled and rubbed his sleeve across his nose, then leaned back against his father's leg. Tears pooled in his eyes, the poor little bugger. Hunter squeezed Eli's shoulders.

She took his hand and held it. "Ye know you can talk to her anytime, right? Each one of you can."

"We can?" Cody pressed himself against Hunter's side.

"Of course you can. You can talk out loud, or keep it secret, in your head. And if you listen real close, you might hear her answer you."

Tripp's eyes grew big. "Nuh-uh."

She smiled at him and leaned forward again. "I talk

to my dad all the time. I really miss him. It helps knowing he's in heaven, watchin' o'er me."

Everything she told them was true. Fifteen years later,
she still missed her da every day. Missed his counsel.
Missed the long walks they used to take. Missed him
even more when her mum had taken off and never come
back.

She stood, and each of the boys hugged her tight.
Seemed she'd made some new friends.

Hunter cleared his throat and looked at his watch.
"You boys need to get back to class."

The boys raced off, hollering *see yas* and *bye, Miss*.

"The resilience of six-year-olds," Hunter said.

"I'm sorry about your loss. I didn't—" She cut her
words off. How could she say *I didn't know you'd lost
your wife, or I wouldn't have been so mean to you*?

Chapter 3

Hunter started his pickup truck and headed to his cabin to get Mackenzie settled. Her words still rang in his head. He'd been struggling for months to know just what to say to the triplets to help them with their grief over losing their mother. And this stranger had come along and got right to the heart of it.

Heck, he was still trying to get over the shock of his ex-wife's death himself. He cleared his throat. "Thanks."

"For what?"

"For what you said to the boys back there."

"I didn't do it for *you*." Icicles could have formed on her words.

An uncomfortable silence descended and he concentrated on the road, tried to figure out what he'd said to tick her off. He usually charmed women. But this one was so different from the type he normally liked.

"I raised my younger brothers after my mum left." Mackenzie's voice was quiet.

"How old were you?"

"I had just turned eighteen. They were all under twelve."

"Didn't you have other family to help?"

"No. And I didn't want them to be split up into foster care."

"Your mom ever come back?"

"She died a year later."

"Oh, man. I'm sorry. I'll bet you did right by them. You're pretty good with kids."

"Th-thanks."

"If you decide you're not cut out for the stuntwoman gig, you could always be a nanny."

Out of the corner of his eye, he saw her head whip toward him. He glanced at her, surprised at the death glare on her face. "What'd I say?"

She huffed, and crossed her arms in front of her, then look out the window.

The temperature *outside* the truck was cold as hell. Suddenly, it felt just as cold inside. *Women.*

When they reached his cabin, he got out, intent on opening her door for her, but she'd already climbed out and grabbed her bags.

So he veered to the front door and unlocked it, stood aside to let her go in, then followed her. "You can have the older section of the cabin."

She stopped suddenly, and he almost plowed into her.

"*This* is a cabin?" She looked up at the vaulted ceiling.

"It used to be much smaller. We added on when the boys came to live with me."

Her head swiveled as she scanned the living room.

He winced, wishing he'd made the boys pick up their toys earlier that morning.

"They didn't live with you?"

"Divorced."

The rigid line of her shoulders relaxed, and she faced him. "And she passed on?"

"Yeah."

"I'm sorry. Had you been divorced long?"

He hesitated.

"Forget I asked. None of my business. Where will I be staying?"

He stepped by her to lead the way to the original master bedroom. "Down this hall." He'd had Kade expand it with the intention of letting Yvette's parents come for longer visits. He had no intention of keeping them from their grandchildren, especially after they lost their only daughter. He'd made sure they knew they were welcome at any time.

The bed faced a wall of windows that overlooked the mountains and lake. Comfy chairs and a small table furnished the room. He walked over to the fireplace and made sure there were plenty of logs. "Plenty of extra blankets in the closet over there, bathroom is through that door."

She set her bags down on the bed. "Thank you. I'll stay out of your way as much as possible."

"Sorry this is the only option. The movie crew is taking up every square inch of space on the ranch."

She opened her mouth to say something, but a shrill ring pierced the heavy tension in the room. He stuck a hand in his pocket for his phone, but realized it was hers.

"Later." He headed to the door and walked out.

Pausing to pull the door closed, he heard her laugh. "Fergus, my luv!"

He shut the door and walked away, wondering what type of man would actually want to be with such a prickly woman, and if Fergus was a boyfriend or husband.

* * *

An hour later, Mackenzie bundled up and left Hunter's cabin. The day was still gray, the clouds hanging low, obscuring the mountains. It reminded her of winter in the Highlands, and her heart ached for home. And her brothers.

Fergus had surprised her with his call. It had been good but painful to hear his voice. She wanted to see her brothers desperately, assure herself they were all happy, healthy and thriving. Fergus had promised her they were all good. The twins were doing great in university, and Ian was dating a new girl.

Hearing Fergus talk about his own girlfriend made Mackenzie feel ancient. He was only twenty-one, for Saint Margaret's sake. Much too young to be serious about anyone. Same with Ian. She decided to scrimp even more, and maybe then she could afford a trip home to see them.

A horn behind her broke the stillness of the day, and she jumped, then scooted off the road. She slipped on a patch of ice and scrambled to right herself. Which made it even worse, and she whomped down on her backside into a melting snowdrift.

The truck brakes squealed to a stop, and a door slammed.

"Mackenzie, are you okay? Are you hurt?" She heard Hunter's voice before she saw him. She looked heavenward and fell back into the snow. *Why did it have to be him?*

"You should be more careful out here." He leaned down, arm outstretched to help her up.

"*I* need to be more careful? *You* need to not blast the bloody horn at unsuspecting people." She jerked her hand away from his grasp.

"Sorry. Why are you out walking in this weather?"

She glared up at him, thrust her hands sideways. "Well, duh. How else am I supposed to get to work?"

"You could have asked me for a ride."

Pushing herself off the ground, she brushed snow off her backside and legs. "I've already inconvenienced you enough." She turned on her heel and headed toward the lodge.

She heard the truck start behind her, and tires crunched on the snow.

"Would you just get in? I'm going the same way as you anyway," Hunter called through the open passenger window.

"Fine," she mumbled. "Bloody, blooming bampot, *man*."

"I heard that," Hunter said. "You wound me, you really do."

She glanced at him, hand pressed against his chest, an exaggerated look of hurt on his face. Despite herself, she laughed.

"I looked it up, you know."

"What?" she asked.

"Bampot."

Her cheeks heated. She felt a touch of remorse, but their interactions to this point flashed through her head, and she stomped it down.

"So who's Fergus? Your husband?"

"What? Why do you ask that?"

"Because your voice sounded like you'd just gotten a puppy on Christmas morning when he called you."

"Not my husband."

"Boyfriend?"

"I don't have a boyfriend."

"Girl as pretty as you should have plenty of boy-friends."

He thought her pretty? "Don't be daft. Fergus is my brother." Searching for a way to change the subject, she remembered the question she'd had earlier while she'd unpacked. "Is there a school on the ranch?"

"No. Oh, for the boys. A lot of the kids on ranches are homeschooled, at least during winter since we're never sure we can get to town. Sometimes special lessons are done via computers, too, as long as the Wi-Fi is up and running."

She looked around at the wooden ranch buildings set against the backdrop of soaring mountains covered in snow. What a wonderful place to grow up.

They arrived at the lodge and got out of the truck.

"What time will you be through today?" he asked.

"I'm not sure. Maybe around seven?"

Hunter handed her a card with several numbers written on it. "Call me or one of these numbers for a ride to my place."

She started to protest, but he held up a hand. "Don't argue. Just do it. It's safe on the ranch, but at night, you never know what wildlife you might run into on the path."

"Thanks. I appreci—" A loud squeal behind her cut her words off.

Carley practically skipped down the path to them and threw her arms around Hunter. "Sweetie! Come have lunch with me."

Now why can't she fall on her bum in front of him? Why did it have to be me? Mackenzie pulled her back-pack over her shoulder.

"Hey, pretty lady." Hunter slung an arm around Carley's shoulders as they walked up the path to the lodge.

Here she'd just started thinking he was nice for call-ing her pretty. She decided he was natural charmer. He'd be that way with women of all ages, all shapes, all types, handing out compliments to anyone of the female per-suasion. Probably even female cats and dogs.

She turned on her heel and walked toward the movie set, scooped up a handful of snow and shaped it into a perfectly round snowball. Aiming at a distant tree, she hefted it through the air. It landed with a soft thud and broke apart in a shower of fragments. She'd do well to re-member Hunter's type, the type her mother had warned her about all those years ago. The type who'd kept break-ing Mum's heart, over and over again.

They're all the same, daughter. They only want one thing—to make you fall in love with them, then they'll break your heart. All you are is another tally mark on their scoreboard.

Mackenzie had learned that lesson the hard way. She'd vowed long ago she'd never fall for any man again. Especially a man like Hunter Sullivan.

Mackenzie dragged herself up the path to the lodge, aching for a cup of tea. She'd gone over and over the upcoming stunt and finally worked out the kinks with Brody, the stunt coordinator. She pressed a hand to her back and stretched. Even as good as it had gone today, fear lingered behind the satisfaction. The fire scene loomed over her head.

"Miss Mackenzie!" a little boy's voice called out to her.

She turned around and saw the triplets racing up the steps toward her, their father following.

"Hey." Hunter tipped his hat to her. "We're going to my dad's house for dinner. Come eat with us."

"Oh, no. I don't want to intrude."

"No intrusion at all. Plenty of food."

"Come on, it'll be fun." Cody grabbed her hand, started pulling her down a sidewalk curving around the outside of the lodge.

"I suppose I could, if you're sure your da won't mind." She looked back at Hunter.

"I don't think the triplets will let you out of it." He grinned.

They followed the walkway to a large cabin. The wood was dark with age, and it looked as if this might have been the original cabin on the property.

Hunter stepped around her and the boys and opened the front door. He gestured for her to precede him, and she walked into a wall of noise.

"Is this a party?" She glanced up at him.

"Nope, just Friday night dinner at my dad's house."

A pretty, older woman with perfectly styled blond hair walked up to their little group. "Hunter, it's about time you and the boys arrived. Dinner is almost ready." She bent over and tapped her cheek, and the triplets pushed and shoved each other to give her a kiss.

Standing back up, she looked at Mackenzie. "Hello, I don't think we've met yet. You're Carley, right?"

Hunter kissed the woman's cheek. "Bunny, this is Mackenzie Campbell. She's actually Carley's stunt double. Mackenzie, my stepmother, Bunny Sullivan."

Mackenzie shook the woman's hand and noticed the questioning eyebrow.

"She's staying at our house," Cody piped up, grinning so big it looked like his face would split.

And there went Mrs. Sullivan's other eyebrow.

"Oh, you're the one—I'm so sorry we didn't have any

other rooms or cabins available for you. If something comes open, we'll get you moved right away."

Mackenzie smiled at her. "Thank you, Mrs. Sullivan."

"Please, call me Bunny."

A tall man with silver hair and a beard to match walked up to them and put his arm around Bunny's waist.

"Mackenzie, this is my husband, Angus. And this—" Bunny gestured toward the others filling the room "—is our family. Hunter, introduce her around."

"Yes, ma'am." Hunter tucked Mackenzie's arm under his and led her into the living room. He stopped by a man and a very pregnant woman.

"Mackenzie, this is my oldest brother, Nash, and his wife, Kelsey. Their daughter, Maddy, is around here somewhere," he said, looking around the room. "Guys, Mackenzie is one of the stunt doubles for the movie."

"Welcome to the ranch," Nash said.

"Thank you. It's a lovely place."

Kelsey's face brightened. "You're Scottish?"

"Aye, that I am." She elbowed Hunter's side. "And thanks for getting the country right the first try, unlike *some* people."

"It's nice to meet you. I hope you get to enjoy the ranch and not have to work all the time." Kelsey rubbed her belly.

"Thank you."

Another tall, attractive man with dark hair joined them.

"Kade, this is Mackenzie. She's the stunt—oh, never mind," Hunter said. "It'll take all night doing it this way."

He pulled her to the center of the room. "Hey, every-one," he called, but the noise level didn't lower at all. He tried whistling, but it didn't make a dent.

Mackenzie raised her fingers to her lips and gave a sharp whistle. Everyone stopped talking.

Hunter stared at her, green eyes popping open wide. "How'd you learn that?"

She grinned. "Four brothers, remember?"

"Awesome. You'll have to teach me how to do that. Hey, everyone, this is Mackenzie Campbell, stuntwoman. Mackenzie, this is the Sullivan family. Follow along. You'll be tested later."

Panic bloomed in her stomach, and she opened her mouth to protest.

"Just kidding." He laughed, the wretch.

"Bloody American," she mumbled, feeling foolish. But at least she relaxed a little.

Hunter raised his arm and pointed. "Bunny is Kelsey's mom. Kelsey came to the ranch last summer, bringing her mom and daughter. She's a physical therapist and runs a program for wounded vets. Their daughter is Maddy, my favorite niece."

"I'm your only niece!" said a wee lass with curly dark hair.

"Well, that's true. But you're still my favorite." He blew her a kiss, then pointed at the other man she'd almost met earlier. "Kade is next in line—he's ranch manager and an architect. Toby over there is his nine-year-old son. Then Wyatt, and his bride, Frankie."

The blond woman smiled and waved at her.

"That cute little guy hanging on Wyatt's leg is her son—their son—Johnny. Wyatt is the ranch foreman, and he can help with anything you need for stunts. Frankie is the money woman."

He pointed at yet another handsome man sitting in a chair by the fire, holding a squirming puppy. "Luke is a few years older than me, married to his job. He's a veterinarian. And saving the best for last." He spread his arms wide. "Me and my boys."

She couldn't help but grin. "Let me guess. You're the precocious one, the favorite—or so you like to tell everyone."

"Hey, she's got your number, bro," Luke said.

Hunter narrowed his eyes. "Okay, so maybe I *will* test you. Point out who is who."

"Challenge accepted." She faced the room again. "Angus and Bunny. Nash, Kelsey, Maddy." She nodded to the next man. "Kade and Toby. Wyatt, Frankie, Johnny. Luke—and I didn't catch the pup's name."

She turned to Hunter and his boys, all watching her expectantly. "Hunter, Cody, Tripp, Eli." She pointed at each boy in turn, then put her hands on her hips. "How'd I do?"

Laughter and catcalls filled the room to bursting.

"Excellent. You got all that in one shot," Kelsey said. "Even the Triples."

"The who?"

"The Triples. Hunter's boys."

"There must be a story behind that name."

Kelsey laughed. "Toby couldn't say *triplets* when they were born, so he called them *triples*, and it stuck."

Hunter leaned close. "How did you get them right the first time?"

"Easy. Cody is in blue, Tripp in red, Eli in green."

Good thing paying attention to details was so important to her job. It'd helped her impress Hunter…not that that should be important or anything.

He looked at her, with something like…respect? "Pretty good. You catch on quick."

"Dinner is ready. Come and sit." Bunny set a bowl of salad on the big table in the middle of the room.

Everyone gathered around the big dining table, and somehow she found herself sitting between two of the Triples and across from Hunter. Dishes were passed, and she'd just taken a bite of fried chicken when Luke cleared his throat.

"Hey, Hunter, isn't Mackenzie the woman you *saved*—" Luke made air quotes with his fingers "—yesterday morning?"

She set the chicken leg down on her plate, finished chewing and carefully wiped her fingers on the linen napkin. "You *saved* me?" She looked Hunter dead in the eye. "*You*. Saved. *Me?*"

"That's the way we heard it." Wyatt set a roll on his son's plate. "Right, bro?"

"Now, that's not what I—" Hunter began.

"Come on and tell us, Mackenzie. Were you relieved to have such a big, strong, handsome cowboy come to your rescue?" Luke smirked.

She glanced at Luke, saw the grin on his face, the wicked gleam in his eye. And just had to play along.

She clutched her hands tight to her chest. "Oh, yes," she simpered, drawing on her inner Carley. "I was ever so relieved he came to my rescue. I don't know what I'd have done if he hadn't saved poor little ol' me." She looked across the table at Hunter and batted her eyelashes fast enough to cause a breeze in the room. "My hero." She sighed deeply, pasting an angelic smile on her face.

Laughter sounded up and down the dining table.

His lips turned up in a slow grin.

She wasn't used to men smiling at her like that. As if she were the main course on a dessert bar.

A slow heat burned up her chest, and she felt as if she'd been punched.

Not good. Not good at all.

Chapter 4

Hunter unloaded the last of the firewood into the bin outside his cabin, then hauled more logs inside.

With a severe snowstorm brewing, his dad had called a halt to all outdoor activities this morning, including movie production. Nash had picked the boys up from class and would be dropping them off soon. Everyone had been told to hunker down and stay inside.

Mrs. Green, the best ranch cook on the planet, and Bunny had sent extra food back with everyone to their cabins. Hunter had already made sure all the fireplace bins in the cabin were stocked with extra logs.

He headed back outside and walked around the cabin, making sure everything had been battened down. Ice had already formed on the trees and bushes. Long icicles hanging from the eaves had frozen into lethal points.

Going around the corner to the older part, he noticed an open window. He walked up to the wall to close it and saw movement inside. *Weird. No one's supposed to be home this time of day.*

Had an intruder slipped inside while he'd been hauling firewood? He hoped it was a person, and not a foraging bear.

He crept forward as quiet as he could and peered through the open window.

A woman stepped out of the tub, and he glimpsed red marks on the backs of her thighs. She turned and faced him.

Boobs.

Naked boobs. Naked legs. Naked body.

His brain finally caught up with his eyes. The woman inside shrieked and tried to cover her body with her hands.

Dammit. Mackenzie.

"What the bloody hell do you think you're doin'? Are you a keeker?"

"Huh?" *Dang. Real smooth, moron.*

"A peeping tom, you idiot." She grabbed a towel and wrapped it around her body.

"Sorry."

"Why are you looking in my window?"

"Um…" He couldn't think. Why was he outside her window?

The silence grew. A drop of water slid down her elbow. Steam rose around her, making her hair even more curly and vibrant. Another drop of water rolled down her throat onto her chest, until it disappeared into her towel-covered cleavage.

Their eyes locked, and he couldn't look away. Her fist clutched the towel tighter in front of her. And here he was, staring at her like a love-starved man. He wouldn't be surprised to discover himself panting like a dog.

Until now, she'd just been a pain in his ass.

Until now, she'd just been another guest on the ranch.

Until now, he hadn't understood what it meant to burn with lust.

An icy crack broke the silence. He looked up just as a giant icicle broke free and plunged down next to him.

"You think icicles can be used to kill vampires?" He hefted it up so she could see.

She stared at him. Her eyes crinkled, her brows following suit. Then her mouth pursed just a bit. "You're crackers. Stark raving blooming crackers."

"I guess Cody's fascination with supernatural bloodsuckers must be rubbing off on me."

"Hunter?"

"Yeah?"

"Go away."

"Oh. Sure." Dang, he really needed to get some brain cells to start firing.

At the sound of shouts from the driveway, he forced his burning body to walk around the corner of the cabin. The boys were home. He needed a few minutes to calm down.

Hell, he needed to lay facedown in the snow to cool off.

He'd acted like a teenage boy first discovering girls.

Except he wasn't a boy. He was a man.

And Mackenzie was a woman.

All woman.

All naked woman.

In his cabin.

He hadn't felt anything like that since...

Ever.

Damn, damn, damn.

He didn't want to know she was beautiful. He didn't want to know how brave she was, raising her younger brothers, and doing all those stunts. He didn't want to know she'd affected his body this way.

Sure, he liked women. But he was a full-time dad now, with kids he needed to focus on.

So, no. He would not be pursuing the pretty lady from Scotland.

Right?

Hunter woke with a start, his room pitch-dark. The blizzard howled outside, the noise reminding him of coyotes and wolves.

Thunder boomed, and he jolted. It'd been a long time since they'd had a thunder snowstorm. He waited, listening for the sounds of his boys dashing to his room to pile in bed with him. It had become their routine any time it thundered.

But no racing feet pounded across wooden floors. They couldn't possibly be sleeping through all the noise. He reached for the switch on his lamp and turned it. Nothing happened. Grabbing the flashlight from his nightstand, he got up and put his robe on, shoved his feet into slippers.

He walked into the family room. Weird lights and shadows caught his attention. Shining his light around the room, he saw blanket-covered lumps and bumps. A fort?

Awesome.

He and his brothers had created huge, elaborate forts back in their day. They'd gotten in trouble using sheets and blankets meant for the guests too many times to count. This one looked so awesome he wanted to get in and play.

The crunch of chips echoed from inside the fort. The boys knew better than to eat snacks without asking first.

"No way. There aren't any ghosts."

"Oh, aye. There are, Cody."

Mackenzie's voice. What was she doing out here?

And with *his* sons? A little fist of jealousy punched him square in the chest. Sure, she was a novelty, a guest in their home. But he was their dad, and he wanted to be there for his kids. The one they turned to when they were happy or sad, scared or excited.

But what if he *wasn't* enough? He woke up every morning with the bone-deep fear he would fail them.

"Have you ever seen 'em?"

"Of course. Scotland is an ancient land. There're ghosties everywhere. When I was a wee lass, my family lived practically at the base of Urquhart Castle, overlooking Loch Ness. Me and my brothers explored every inch of the castle, ghosts and all."

"How many are there? Are they mean?" Eli's voice squeaked.

"Dozens and dozens. They'd float and flit through the castle, moaning and screaming, so you couldn't count them all."

Hunter grinned. Her voice lowered into spooky tones, and her accent thickened as she told her story.

"Did you go in the castle?"

"Och, aye. I wasna' afraid of some ghosties. Until that one dreadful day that my brothers dared me to go in all alone…and spend the *night*."

"No way!" Eli squeaked.

"Nuh-uh!" Tripp scoffed, but Hunter knew he was loving the story.

"Cool!" That had to be his bloodthirsty Cody.

"What happened next?"

"Well—" she lowered her voice even more, and Hunter leaned forward to listen "—I crept in at midnight, with just a blanket and a candle. I made it into the keep with no troubles. I started going up the old stone steps when I heard it."

"What?" Eli's voice was pitched high, as if the spirit in Mackenzie's story had goosed him.

"The first ghost whooshed down the staircase at me. I ducked, and it flew over my head. A second ghost came right after it, and I swear it flew straight through my body. It was so frightful cold, my fingers turned blue! Then it turned right around and came at me again, screaming and moaning my name."

One of the boys squealed, and Hunter felt left out, wanted to join the fun. He crept forward and yanked up the blanket, sticking his flashlight under his chin. "Boo!"

The boys screamed, and even Mackenzie squeaked.

"Can I come in and play?" He glanced at her. He hadn't seen her since he'd accidentally stared at her through the bathroom window earlier. She'd made herself scarce at dinnertime.

He'd thought he would feel awkward, but right this moment, he didn't. Maybe because of the dark.

But in the glow of all the flashlights, it looked like her cheeks were full-blown red.

"Daddy, she's telling us a ghost story." Cody squirmed in his seat.

Hunter crawled in. The only spot open was next to Mackenzie, and when he brushed her arm, she went rigid and leaned as far away from him as she could.

Too bad.

His house.

His kids.

His rules.

Sure they could roughhouse. But there would be no *adult* games with Mackenzie.

Period.

He had to concentrate on the boys.

Chapter 5

Mackenzie woke up slow and snuggled closer to the heat source. Half her body felt warm, the other cold. Her brain started functioning, and she rubbed her head against the pillow.

Only it wasn't a pillow. It was a hard shoulder.

Attached to a man.

A warm man. In pajamas.

His scent tickled her nose, and she wanted to snuggle into his bathrobe and breathe him in. Her eyes popped open.

The image of seeing him outside the bathroom just as she was getting out of the tub the day before rampaged through her head. She'd grabbed the towel as soon as she saw him, but he had to have seen something.

Oh, bugger it.

She rolled off him, hoping she wouldn't wake him up.

His hand tightened around her shoulder, then he yanked his arm away from her so fast she fell backward onto the cushions.

"Sorry," he whispered.

"I didn't mean to fall asleep in here."

"Hey, you work hard, and it was a long day, late night."

She looked at the triplets sprawled across the cushions and smiled. They were really good boys, and she'd had a marvelous time with them the night before. But now she had to get moving. She crawled out of the fort and into the chilly living room. Weak light filtering through the tall windows meant it was still quite early, maybe still snowing.

She really wanted to lock herself in her room. But with the power off, there was no comforting noise from the heater, and it was freezing in the cabin. She stared at the fireplace, the logs waiting in the bin nearby. The matches sat on the mantel, high enough the boys couldn't get to them.

The boys. They'd need some warmth as soon as they got up. She hesitated, then rubbed her arms up and down to quell the prickles. Living in LA, she hadn't had to worry about building fires. Here? A different story.

But she couldn't let this newfound fear of flames scare her the rest of her life. She was a professional—she would face her fears and do the stunt…with a lot of prayers beforehand. Taking a deep breath, she reached for a log to place on the ashes.

Hunter crawled out behind her. "I'll get it going." He held his hand out for the log.

"I'll take care of it." She moved the log away from him, intent on proving to herself she could do it.

"You're my guest, I'll do it." He pulled at the other end of the log.

"You're kind enough to put me up in your home. I can build the fire."

"Do you know how?"

"Of course I do. I grew up in the Scottish Highlands. I learned at a wee age." Now he'd gone and made her crabbit. She yanked, and the wood slid along her palm, a sharp splinter piercing it. She let go, jerking back. Examining the skin, she spied the offending splinter, blood oozing around it.

"What happened?" He leaned forward and took her hand in his—his very warm, rough, masculine hand.

"Just a splinter." She took a few steps back and tried to breathe again. He was all rumpled and drowsy and very attractive. Too attractive.

"See? You should have let me do it. Come in the kitchen, I have a first-aid kit."

She remembered her da digging in her palm with a pocketknife. She jerked her hand behind her. "No."

"What's wrong? Scared of a little iodine?" He grinned at her.

"Don't be daft. It's just a little splinter."

"At least let me get you tweezers and alcohol to clean it out."

"Oh, fine." She blew her hair out of her eyes. They walked toward the kitchen, and she glanced in the mirror. Curls sprang up everywhere, and a crease marred her cheek. She rubbed at it, then tried to smooth her wayward hair. She may not be attracted to the arrogant man, but she darn sure didna' want him to think her a fright.

He lit a couple of oil lanterns and some candles. Then he pointed at a stool beside the counter, and she sat. Opening a cabinet door, he pulled a white first-aid box out and handed it to her.

She took care of the splinter while he got the fire going again in the other room. Setting the tweezers down, she looked around the kitchen, noting the homey touches. Lighter wood cabinets, granite counters, and children's drawings covered the fridge. A big table sat in a bay window alcove with bench seating and chairs with bright cushions.

He walked back into the kitchen a few minutes later. "How did you end up with my kids in a fort?"

"I'd gotten up for some water, and they came racing downstairs. Cody said the other two were scared of the thunder, and that just escalated into fisticuffs. Then the power snapped out. So I told them we could build a fort and camp out by the fireplace. I hope you don't mind."

He pulled a bag of coffee beans out of the cabinet. "Nah. They usually find me during storms. I haven't wanted to tell them not to." His voice turned a wee bit gruff.

"Your boys are pure brilliant. You and their mother have done well by them."

"Their mom was great with them. We divorced when they were a year old and shared custody as much as possible. They're all her."

"I see a lot of you in them."

He looked up at her, and the hope on his face surprised her.

"You really are doing a bang-up job with them. It's tough raising children after a loss." She hoped he believed her. "I can tell they know they're loved."

"I've had a lot of help from my family."

She opened her mouth to ask more about them, then realized he was making coffee in an electric pot. "When did the power come back on?"

"I turned the generator on."

"So we have power now?"

"Yeah." He looked at her—the *duh*, clearly implied.

"Why didn't you say anything?"

He grinned. "More fun playing it's still off—kind of like camping out."

Despite herself, she laughed. A chime sounded from her phone, and she pulled it out to read a text from the production assistant. "Looks like I get a snow day today. Production is still shut down."

Hunter looked out the windows, and she followed his gaze. Snow still fell from the sky at an alarming pace. At this rate, they'd have to reschedule the scenes where she would ride across the valley.

"Looks like we're all in for a snow day." Hunter grinned, and she swore his expression was a cross between a schoolboy intent on making mischief—and a grown man intent on making mischief…with a woman.

The wind whistled through the trees, echoing in the rafters of the cabin. Icy tremors skipped along her neck, and she pulled her robe up higher. "I'll be back in a tick."

She popped up from the stool, causing it to screech across the floor. Passing by the fort where the kids still slept, she hurried to the opposite side of the cabin to her temporary room. She closed the door and leaned against it. Why was her heart beating so fast?

Hunter had a way of looking at her like she was the only woman on earth. He'd flirt with her in the morning, then flirt with Carley in the afternoon. He was just a natural born flirt. It was his way; it didn't mean anything.

She needed to keep that knowledge front and center. It wouldn't do to get too involved and end up with a broken heart again.

She didn't need a man.

Especially some flirty cowboy from Montana.

So she'd laugh, maybe flirt back a little. But when the job on this film ended, so would her relationship—no, not relationship. Flirtation.

* * *

Hunter scooped the last pancake off the stove as Mackenzie walked back in dressed in jeans and a blue sweater, her hair pulled back in a ponytail. Too bad. She'd looked cute in her pajamas and robe, her red hair wild.

Now her armor was back on, shielding her marshmallow insides. And the trim body he'd seen the day before. He'd had more than one dream about her last night—especially after she'd snuggled up to him while she slept in the fort.

But she was a guest in his home, a paying guest on their ranch. Besides, she was as prickly as a cactus, and he didn't want to get stabbed. Best just to forget about her body. Not like they could do anything with three miniature chaperones underfoot anyway.

"Breakfast is ready." He set the pancakes down on the kitchen table with a flourish. One of the few meals he could actually prepare without trouble. He pulled a chair out opposite the bench seat and held it for her.

Mackenzie hesitated, and he cocked his head, waiting till she finally moved forward and sat.

Looked like her skittishness had come back. He wondered if it was all men, or just him that made her so shy. And why? Had someone hurt her in the past?

He passed the platter around, made sure Tripp didn't take too many, and that Eli had enough. The syrup bottle made its way around in silence, and as he took it from Mackenzie, their fingers touched. An electric shock so big he could see it sparked between their fingers, and she jerked back.

"What was that?" She rubbed the back of her hand.

"Dry air?" He felt as surprised as she looked.

Their eyes collided for a brief moment. The boys

started shoving each other, fighting over the last pancakes.

She ate in silence, but he wanted to draw her out for some reason. It wasn't often he couldn't charm a woman.

Not that he intended it to go anywhere. "Is Mackenzie a family name?"

"Aye. My grandmother's maiden name."

He thought back to the night before, the stories she'd been telling. "You said you grew up near Loch Ness?"

She nodded.

"Did you ever see the Loch Ness *Monster*?" He pitched his voice louder over the boys' ruckus.

They immediately stopped shoving and shouting, and stared at Mackenzie.

Eli's hand jerked sideways, and left a trail of syrup from his plate to the table. "What monster? Where?"

"In Scotland, where Miss Mackenzie grew up," Hunter told them.

"Where's Scotland?" Cody mumbled around a mouthful of pancake.

"Well now, lad, it's all the way across the globe from here."

"How about if we get the big map out later and she can show you?" Hunter wiped syrup off the table.

"There's monsters in Scotland?" Tripp asked, impatient with the geography lesson on a snow day.

"Aye, there are." Mackenzie took another bite of pancake.

"No there's not," Tripp said. The oldest by six minutes, he took his role very seriously. Always the first to shout hogwash.

"I've seen Nessie with my very own eyes." She opened her eyes extra wide.

"What's it look like?" Cody asked.

"She's a giant creature, like a monstrous big snake or a dinosaur, only she lives in the loch near my home."

"What's a loch?" Eli asked.

"Loch is Scottish for lake. The legend goes way back, over a thousand years to the very first sighting of Nessie in the waters. Rumor has it a farmer got too close, and Nessie snatched him right up and ate him." She shoved a bite of bacon in her mouth and made chomping noises.

Hunter realized he'd leaned forward as much as the boys. Her accent thickened as she spoke. Mackenzie had a real knack for storytelling.

"One day I was walking home from school. It was cold and blustery, and the wind ripped my hat right off my head, sent it winging down to the loch. I gave my books to my brother Fergus and chased after it. The closer I got to the loch, the darker and spookier it got."

Every eye around the table was glued to Mackenzie.

"Just as I reached the rocks at the shoreline, the water started churning and bubbling, like a witch's cauldron. Up rose a head, higher, higher, higher, then a very long neck, almost like a giant sea snake. The scales were dark green, and so shiny they hurt my eyes. Nessie turned and looked at me, her eyes glittering."

"Then what?" Cody asked, impatient for the gory details.

"My hat blew right over the water, all the way up, until it hit Nessie right smack on the nose. My da had paid good money for that hat, and I didn't want to leave it behind. He'd be fierce mad at me for losing it."

The boys were quiet for once, hanging on every word.

"But Nessie looked so ferocious, I'd frozen like a block of ice, too scared to go after it. Then her mouth opened and she roared, louder than all the lions in Africa. Her teeth were like sharp spikes of steel, and seaweed and water dripped from her jaw. She roared again, and I turned and ran as fast as I could, all the way home."

"Did she chase you?" Cody asked.

Mackenzie shook her head. "Nay, not that day. But you know what happened the next morning? I got ready for school and opened the door. And there, hooked on the fence post—can you guess what it was?"

"A dead fish?" Eli asked.

She leaned forward. "Nope. Even spookier."

"The dead farmer?" Cody leaned forward, too, his Batman pajamas almost touching his plate.

Hunter slid his eyes to Mackenzie, and saw her bite her lip to keep from laughing.

"It was…my…*hat*!"

"No way!" Tripp shouted.

"Way." She picked up her fork and took another bite of pancake.

"Cool." Cody sat back, and Hunter could almost see the thoughts whirring in his head.

"Are there more monsters? Did you see any?" Eli asked.

"Scotland is a mystical, magical land. There are many supernatural creatures, so many it would take weeks and weeks to tell you about."

"You boys finished eating? We need to get the dishes cleaned up." Hunter stood and picked up his plate.

"Aw, Daddy. Puhleeze? We wanna hear more, Miss Mkeznie," Eli begged, garbling her name.

"Why don't you call me Mack? That's what my brothers call me." She stood and started picking up plates.

"Miss Mack, Miss Mack, Miss Mack," Cody sang at the top of his lungs.

"Okay, Miss Mack." Tripp got up and shoved Cody.

"We'll take care of the dishes." Hunter took the stack

of dishes from her hand. "Thanks for the story. You've got a great way with kids."

Her cheeks turned pink, and she started walking out of the kitchen.

"Mackenzie." He waited till she turned around. "I enjoyed the story, too. I wouldn't mind hearing more sometime." He grinned at her.

And she fled the room as if the Loch Ness Monster was hot on her heels.

Chapter 6

Mackenzie took a deep breath of crisp mountain air. She'd had a bad case of cabin fever, aching to get outside again. Sure, it had been fun playing games with the triplets, even when Hunter joined in. But she'd needed some time by herself, so she worked on her newest hobby—jewelry making.

The weather had finally cleared enough they could film outdoors again. Today they were shooting the scene in which the hero and heroine were lost in the wilderness, snowbound by the aftermath of a blizzard.

At least Mother Nature cooperated yesterday by dumping heaps and heaps of snow.

Mackenzie zipped up the thick coat that matched what Carley wore. Everything had to be the exact duplicate, down to their hairstyles. She pulled on gloves and headed toward the van equipped with tracks to ride over snow that would take them to the film location.

"Yo, Mackenzie." Steven, the lead actor's stunt double, caught up to her.

Mackenzie hadn't worked with Steven before. She'd

heard he was the nephew of some big producer who had pulled strings to get him this job. She really hoped he knew what the was doing, otherwise someone could get hurt. They'd been closeted with the stunt coordinator and the assistant director that morning, going over procedures.

She glanced at Steven, then behind him. Hunter walked out of the barn, leading his horse. His sons followed him, each with smaller horses of their own.

"Hey, you listening to me?" Steven slung an arm around her shoulders. "I haven't seen you for a few days."

"We need to get moving." She shrugged out from under his arm, and saw Hunter watching them. She waved at the boys, and Eli waved so hard his hat fell off. Cody took his hat off and waved it. Tripp grinned at her.

Climbing into the van, she made sure to take the single seat in the back so *I'm-God's-gift-to-women* Steven wouldn't sit next to her. The driver took the crew out to the edge of a field overlooking a ravine, and they all disembarked.

After hours of blocking and rehearsing, the director called *action*, and she held still, watching Carley and Bryant as they trudged through the snow. Desperate to find shelter after their plane had crashed, and having no one else to turn to, they would end the scene with an argument about which way to go. The script called for Carley to peer over a ravine, then lose her footing and slide down toward the freezing river.

The camera stopped rolling, and Mackenzie walked out to take Carley's place. The wind whipped her hair around her head and blew snow up into her eyes. She tucked her chin down into the warm red wool scarf while Brody attached the harness to her safety belt.

She shuffled forward to look over the ravine. A steep drop from the rocky crag ended in a wide river lined with boulders. A second camera crew had set up on a narrow strip of land to film her as the character fell over the edge and slid down the ravine. Tom had found a pathway down to the water and hurried toward the crew. He'd mentioned wanting to watch the stunt for real, not just on a monitor.

Mackenzie waited for the cue to begin her downward slide.

"Action!" Tom's voice sounded tinny as he spoke through a radio.

She went to work. Sliding her foot forward, she felt for the soft spot and pushed. The edge of the cliff gave way like they'd planned. Her arms flew up as she tumbled down the cliff. Sharp rocks poked at her, and spikes of adrenaline shot through her stomach and chest. She scrambled for a handhold, but with the snow and ice so deep, any brush she could have grabbed was buried. Perfect for what the script called for.

Halfway down the slope, the harness yanked her to a stop. One of the straps dug into her stomach, right over a scar. Her skin was still sensitive, and she bit her lip against the reminder of the fire.

The crew high above started lowering her down, and she finally touched the ground. Brushing the snow off her hands and face, she waited while the director watched the playback on the screen.

"Great job, Mackenzie. You made that fall look realistic. Should be good to go on this stunt," Tom said, and gave her a thumb's up.

"Thanks." She kept her face calm, gave a slight smile. But inside she jumped up and down. *Woohoo!* Always a relief to have a stunt go right. And on the first try, too.

She walked into the crew tent to warm herself at the space heaters. The lead actor, Bryant, stood at the back getting some coffee, and Carley looked up at Mackenzie.

"I hear you're staying at Hunter's cabin." Carley set a script down on a small table.

"Aye, that's correct."

Carley glanced at Bryant, then pulled a small compact out of her pocket and looked in the mirror. "I hope you're not getting any ideas about him. It won't go anywhere."

Mackenzie's jaw tightened. "I don't know what you mean."

"Just in case you're thinking he'll go for you, he won't. We've been seeing each other since I arrived." Carley snapped the compact closed.

Bryant brushed past them and tossed his cup in the trash. He yanked the tent flap open and shot a look at Carley, then walked out.

"You forget I was snowbound with him in his cabin during the blizzard." Sometimes Carley irritated her so much. The actress thought the world revolved around her.

"You—" Carley jumped up out of the director's chair emblazoned with her name.

"Oh, relax. He's no more interested in me than I am in him." Mackenzie walked to the tent flap and held it aside. "Besides, we had three chaperones, remember? His boys?"

She pushed through the tent and walked outside. Why would Carley think she had any interest in Hunter? Although, it had been very tempting to let Carley know Hunter had seen her naked.

The assistant director hailed her. *Time to go back to work.* She had to stand in for Carley as they filmed Bryant's reaction scenes. This was the boring part. She could lose herself while Bryant ran his lines for the camera's close-up shots.

She loved action work best. Flying through the air, swinging from a harness, riding on top of a semi, hanging off a cliff. It was more than just a rush of adrenaline. For years, she'd felt the most like herself during stunts.

Since before she'd realized she could never again rely on a man to make her happy, to make her feel alive. Doing stunt work, *she* was in control.

Thirty minutes later, she'd finished standing in for Carley. Instead of waiting to ride back with the crew, she opted to walk the couple of miles back to the ranch to begin laying out the next stunt. And thaw out her frozen toes in a warm bath.

She trudged down the road, the warm scarf pulled up to her nose. An engine sounded behind her, and she moved off the road, trying to avoid the muddy patches.

One of the smaller ranch snow coaches pulled up alongside her and stopped. The window rolled down, and one of Hunter's brothers—Luke?—poked his head out.

"Hey, Mackenzie. Need a ride?"

"Sure, that would be grand."

He shoved the passenger door open and she grabbed the handrail, hauling herself inside.

"Where you headed? Back to Hunter's cabin?"

"The barn by the lodge, please. I want to check on my horse."

Luke put the big machine in gear, and they rolled forward over the snowy road. "So you like doing stunts in movies?"

"Aye. I can pay bills doing something I love." The only thing she hated now were scenes involving fire. At least she wouldn't be trapped in a box this time. She just hoped she wouldn't freeze up and not be able to do it. She didn't want to gain a bad rep.

"You played along great the other night at dinner."

Luke's words interrupted her dark thoughts. "Oh, you mean about Hunter *saving* me?"

"Yeah. We take every opportunity to mess with him."

And they had. Every one of his brothers had poked fun at him. "And he goes along with that?"

Luke shrugged. "Doesn't matter. He's too pretty for his own good, so we have to take him down a notch whenever we can."

She started feeling sorry for Hunter, and felt bad for her part in the raucous teasing that night.

"Don't get me wrong. He's our brother, and all. Sometimes it's just too much to resist." Luke steered the snow coach to the barn. "Believe me, he dishes it out just as much."

Grinning, she opened the door. "Understood." She slid out of the coach. "Thanks for the lift." She walked into the barn and over to Rory's stall. "Hi, handsome." She rubbed his nose.

Rory nudged her shoulder, then her pocket. She laughed and opened the stall door and went in. He always knew when she'd brought him a treat. She pulled the apple out of her pocket, but he shifted and bumped into her. The apple fell from her hand, and she bent over to pick it up.

The barn door creaked open, and with the burst of cold air came the sound of Carley's flirty laugh.

"Hunter, you naughty boy." She squealed, then laughed again.

Hunter's voice rumbled, but his words weren't clear enough for Mackenzie to hear what he said. More than likely, he was whispering sweet nothings into Carley's ear.

Just like a man. Wink at her in the morning, seduce another woman in the afternoon.

She wondered who would be on his radar for that evening.

Oh, well, none of her business. It wasn't as if *she* was interested in him. She had a job to do, and she needed to do it perfectly. If the weather held out a few more days, her part would be done, and she could leave and look for another stunt job.

The coordinators, and especially Brody, were good about telling her who was hiring stunt people, but sometimes it felt as if all she did was hustle for work.

Carley laughed again, and it sounded like the one she used for her romantic scenes. That hot and sultry laugh that made Mackenzie think about Elizabeth Taylor. The barn door slammed shut.

A little trickle of something pinged around her chest. Not jealousy. *Absolutely not*. A man like Hunter would never look at her as anything more than a pal, a buddy. Especially when pretty, feminine Carley was in the vicinity.

And no skin off her own freckled nose. She wasn't here for romance.

Mackenzie fed the apple to Rory, and took extra time to brush him as a treat. She hung up the brush, kissed him on the nose, filled up his feed bucket and gave him clean water. "Good night, *mo charaid.*" She made sure he was secure, then walked out of the barn and closed the door.

The wind blew a dusting of snow into her face, and she wrapped the scarf around herself more securely. The sun had already started setting by the time she walked the distance to Hunter's cabin.

Ready for a hot bath, then to settle down with her notes for her next scene, she opened the front door to the cabin, but stopped when a pickup truck pulled into the driveway.

Nash got out and helped the boys down. The Triples

raced toward her, shoving each other aside to give her the first hug.

Nash limped up the walkway, looking at his phone. He stopped abruptly and ran a hand over his chin. Even from the doorway she could tell something was wrong. He hurried the rest of the way to her.

"Mackenzie, tell Hunter I can't stay after all. Kelsey just texted she's having pains. I have to go." He didn't wait for a response, but turned and limped back to his truck and got in. The engine roared to life and he sped off around the corner.

The boys had already raced inside, and she followed them. She hoped Kelsey would be okay. They had only briefly talked the other night, but she really liked the other woman.

"Dad's not here!" Cody said to her as she walked into the big living room.

That was odd. Nash had sounded like he was supposed to be meeting Hunter here. "I'll text him." She pulled out her phone and texted him to let him know the boys were there, and that Nash couldn't stay.

She didn't have to wait long for an answer.

In mtg. Can u watch them?

A slow burn started in her stomach. How dare he treat her like a babysitter! Another text interrupted her inner rant.

Pretty please? Won't be long. Will owe you. Big time.

A string of emoticons followed, with hearts and kisses. She laughed. Always the flirt.

Fine. But it'll cost you. Big-time. She sent the text,

then remembered hearing him and Carley in the barn. Was he really at a meeting?

At the sound of shouting, she hurried upstairs. She hadn't ventured to the upper floor yet, not wanting to be a snoop.

Walking through one of the open doorways, she stopped and stared. The bedroom and play area took up almost the entire second story. There were three loft beds made of dark wood, each outfitted with a narrow staircase instead of a ladder. Beneath each bunk sat a pint-size desk and chair. Shelves ran across one short wall, floor to ceiling, and were filled with books and games.

Big windows overlooked the trees, mountains and lake. The walls had been painted to look like trees, the shelves like tree branches. Leafy green accents dotted the room, with a mural of Montana wildlife painted on one wall. It was like living in a huge treehouse, and she loved it. Her brothers would have loved it, too.

The boys were running around as if they'd been supercharged on sugar. Toys were flung hither and yon, and her head started hurting from the noise.

She caught Cody as he ran by her, but he wiggled away when she reached for Tripp. He got away from her, too, and she'd finally had enough. Using the whistle that always stopped her brothers in their tracks, she was happy to see it worked the same on these little American heathens.

"Is this how you act when your da is not around?"

Tripp shrugged from where he sat, holding Eli in a weird wrestling position.

"Why don't you boys grab a book and read?"

"No way! School is over!" Cody piped up.

"A game?" she asked, hoping against hope.

Eli shoved Tripp off him and raced around the room.

She really needed to get a workout in—she'd missed it the day before. She cocked her head. Maybe they could join her and use up some of that energy at the same time.

"I need to practice my stunts. You boys want to learn some?"

They all stopped and looked at each other, then at her. "Yes!"

"Brilliant," she mumbled to herself. "Gather the pillows off your bed and lay them out here." She pointed where she wanted them placed. "I'll be right back." She hurried down to her room and changed into yoga pants and a fitted tee. Jogging back up the steps to the boys' room, she hoped they hadn't done anything too crazy in the few minutes she was gone.

"Have any of you taken tumbling classes or gymnastics?"

"Gymnastics is for girls." Tripp wiped his sleeve across his nose.

She put her hands on her hips. "You think so? What's your favorite action movie?"

"Spider-Man!" they all shouted loud enough to shake the rafters.

"So remember how Spider-Man leaps and jumps and flies from rooftops and buildings all over town?"

They boys nodded.

She walked to one side of the playroom with plenty of space and turned to face them.

Running a few steps, she leaped through the air, landed, tucked into a tumble, hopped up immediately into a handspring and flipped herself over to land on her feet.

She ended up at the opposite side of the room and turned around to see the boys gaping at her, eyes so wide they looked like a caricature of pugs.

"Is that girlie?" she asked, hands on hips.

"How'd you do that?" Tripp asked.

"Teach me!" Eli hollered.

"Whoaaaaa," Cody drawled.

"I learned how to somersault when I was just about your age. And now I can do all of this. And you know what?" She crooked her finger to beckon them closer. "I get paid to have fun doing tumbling."

"Cool!" the boys shouted.

"So who wants to learn how to somersault?"

They spent the next hour tumbling all over the room, with the pillows there to keep them safe. The next hour she graduated them into handstands.

She got the boys all situated in expert—for the most part—handstands using the wall for support. Bending over to fall into a freestanding handstand, she glanced at the big clock on the wall and noticed how much time had passed. Hunter had promised to be home soon—looked like that was one promise he'd broken rather quickly.

Yes, she'd had fun with the triplets. But she'd already raised four boys. She had a job to do here, and it wasn't to be a nanny. Especially if he was out seeing Carley and not actually working.

Hunter tossed his briefcase on the sofa, then set the bags down on the kitchen counter. Bone-deep tired, frustrated and with a rare headache blooming behind his eyes. The only thing good that had come out of the business meeting was it had given him an escape from Carley. She'd caught him unawares earlier at the barn, and while he hadn't wanted to hurt her feelings, he really wasn't up for her flirting. It had started grating on his nerves.

Thumps and shouts from the second floor sent a jolt

of panic through his stomach. He ran up the steps and into the boys' room.

Pillows were strewed across the floor, and his boys were all standing against the wall—on their hands.

Mackenzie—she stood on her hands in the middle of the room, talking to the boys in her thick accent. She made it look effortless, casually balancing on her hands, her wild red curls cascading upside down to the floor, her olive green T-shirt riding up to show a patch of creamy skin.

He kept quiet, wondering how long they had been that way. The seconds ticked by, and she still talked to them, telling a story about a movie she'd done stunts in. The boys all laughed, and Eli fell over onto a pillow, laughing so hard he clutched his stomach. As he sat up, he spotted Hunter in the doorway.

"Daddy! Did you see me? Did you see me?" Eli hollered, racing to hug him.

Mackenzie wobbled, then lowered her legs and flipped up to her feet. She yanked her T-shirt over her stomach, her face a bright red. He wondered if it was from the blood rushing to her head, or embarrassment at being caught red-handed, so to speak.

"I did see you. How'd you all learn to do handstands?" he asked, squeezing Eli close.

Mackenzie helped Cody and Tripp down from their positions, and the boys ran over to hug him.

"We had a blast, Daddy! Miss Mack taught us how to pretend we were Spider-Man in the movies," Cody shouted.

"Tell her thank-you, boys."

They all ran over to hug Mackenzie now. "Thank you, thank you," they shouted.

Sometimes he thought the volume control for their inside voices had been stuck on high.

"Go get washed up for dinner, then come downstairs," he told the boys. "And hang up the towels," he hollered over their thundering feet.

He turned around to thank Mackenzie, but she'd already disappeared through the doorway. By the time he reached the bottom of the stairs, she was gone. Changing his route, he went to the kitchen to get dinner ready.

Thirty minutes later, the boys roared downstairs and skidded into the kitchen. He got plates and utensils out, and they set the table.

"One of you go get Miss Mackenzie for dinner."

Thus proceeded a skirmish, shouting, shoving and shrieking, until he couldn't stand it any longer. "Quiet!" He added his own shout to the mix. At least this time it was loud enough to quiet them down.

He pointed the slotted spoon at Cody. "You. Go get Miss Mack."

The other two boys muttered, mumbled, pouted and grumbled.

"Sit," he ordered. Among chairs screeching over the wooden floor, they finally sat.

"I got her!" Cody shouted, coming back into the kitchen, dragging Mackenzie by the hand.

Hunter nodded, wincing at the volume. "Cody, sit." He glanced at Mackenzie, now shrouded in an overly large dark green sweatshirt that said University of Aberdeen on the front.

She walked over to the counter. "You don't have to feed me again. I can go to the lodge and eat with the crew."

"No trouble. You're here. It's cold out. Besides…" He

leaned closer. "I need to apologize for imposing on you to watch the boys. I'm sorry."

"About that. I didna' mind—too much—but I'm here to work. I can't be a nanny—"

"I promise it was a onetime thing. I was in a real bind. I'm still trying to learn how to juggle being a full-time dad with work—and with Kelsey…" He broke off, worried for his sister-in-law, worried about being a good dad, worried he'd screw up his kids forever.

"Have you heard if she's okay?"

"They called the doctor. She's better now, Nash thinks. Anyway, thank you." He pulled a pan out of the oven. "Would you like some wine with dinner?"

She glanced at him, then at the table. "I'd love some milk, like the boys are having."

He barely refrained from raising his eyebrow, but got another glass out of the cabinet and handed it to her.

She sat and poured milk into the glass, then turned it around. "I see you broke out the fancy stemware for dinner."

"Huh?"

She held up the glass, and he wanted to sink into the floor. He'd inadvertently grabbed a glass from the boys' Disney collection for her.

He walked to the table, hand outstretched. "I'll get you a new one."

"Nay." She took a sip. "She'll do just fine for me."

His lips quirked up in a crooked grin, and his headache started to fade. "Hey, at least the character is the redheaded girl from that Scottish movie."

He grabbed the pan from the top of the stove and brought it to the table, handed the serving spoon to Mackenzie. "Guests first. Go ahead and serve yourself."

Stretching sideways, he grabbed the basket of corn

bread muffins and the butter, then sat down just as she leaned over and picked up a piece of paper off the floor. She glanced at it, then set it on the table.

"Is this mince and tatties?" She scooped up a forkful and took a bite.

"Excuse me?"

She pointed at the dish. "It looks like mince and tatties. It's a staple in our house at home in Scotland."

"Shepherd's pie. The boys love it."

"Whatever you Americans call it, it's very good." She ate another bite, then took a muffin from the basket and buttered it.

"Glad you like it." He closed his eyes and put his wrist against his forehead. "I slaved over a hot stove."

The boys all hooted with laughter, and he opened his eyes to see Mackenzie smirking at him.

"You mean your saintly Mrs. Green slaved over the hot stove."

"Why, I'm wounded, I truly am. You don't think I could make a great dinner?"

She held up the paper. "'From the kitchen of Mrs. Green. Warm in a three-hundred-fifty-degree oven for…' Shall I continue reading the instructions?"

"Dad, you're busted!" Tripp shouted.

Mackenzie laughed and crumpled the paper, then chucked it at his head.

"Okay, okay. I'll admit she sent dinner home with me. But only because the meeting ran late."

"Yeah, or he'd have made peanut-butter-and-jelly sammiches for dinner." Cody snickered.

"Oh, you think so, pal?" Hunter leaned over and scrubbed his knuckles over Cody's head. "How about you, Miss Mackenzie. Do you cook?"

She sat up straighter in her chair. "I'll have ye know

I'm a verra good cook. Maybe I'll cook for you lot one night."

"What do you cook where you come from?" Eli asked.

"All kinds of dishes. But my brothers especially love my haggis."

"Haggis? What's that?" Tripp asked around a mouthful of food.

"It's the national food of Scotland. Every good Scot loves it," she said, a twinkle in her eye as she looked at each of the boys.

"Haggis has onions, hearty oats, delicious spices, garden-grown herbs and—" she leaned forward "—sheep's heart, liver and lungs, all sewn up in the sheep's stomach." She sat back and rubbed her stomach and made *nummy nummy* noises.

"Gross!" Tripp piped up. "You made that up."

She shook her finger. "I would ne'er do that about something so sacred to the Scottish people."

"What'd you call it again?" Eli asked.

"Haggis."

His sons then proceeded to repeat the word, each time saying it with increasing gagging noises.

"Thanks for that," he said to her over the noise.

She shrugged. "I told you you'd owe me big-time. Consider this the first installment." Picking up her glass of milk, she took a sip, her eyes sparkling with laughter.

He pointed his fork at her. "Well done, my Scottish miss, well done. What's next on your agenda to make me pay?"

She set her glass down. "I'll be thinkin' on that tonight as I go to sleep. Count on it."

"Then I'll be thinking about all the ways you could make me pay as I go to sleep tonight," he said, surprised at how her words suddenly sounded flirtatious. He liked it.

A red flush rushed up her neck to almost cover her face, and she nearly toppled her milk as she set the glass down.

He watched her, betting anything she was fighting the urge to get up and run away from him.

Far and fast, maybe even all the way back to Scotland.

Chapter 7

The next evening, Mackenzie let Cody, Tripp and Eli drag her out of the cabin and to the big coach waiting to take them to the lodge. She'd wanted to collapse into bed. A sleepless night before, tossing and turning all night thinking about Hunter lying in *his* bed, thinking about *her*, had kept her restless and unsettled.

Honestly, other men had flirted with her before and she'd been able to shut them down, shut them out of her mind. She'd learned her lesson but good on the first movie she'd worked on in the US. She'd been alone, and lonely, no friends or family, so she had liked the attention the lead actor had shown her. It wasn't till after he'd succeeded in making her fall for him, *and* taken her to bed, that she found out he'd done it on a dare. He didn't really care about *her*, just ticking one more female off his list.

And now Hunter…

He was on her mind, under her skin, making her itchy, twitchy and downright witchy.

The more she tried to shut him down, the harder he tried to win her over.

Why couldn't he understand she wasn't there to play with him? She had to do a job, and do it well. Keep her mind focused, especially at work. It wouldn't do to end up injured again—either her heart or her body.

He was great with his kids, but more than once she'd noticed a little wrinkle of worry creasing his forehead. Like the one she'd seen way too many times on her own forehead after Mum had left them, then died a year later, and it was up to her to raise her brothers.

The Triples chattered and shoved, each trying to outdo the other, all the way to the lodge. They finally pulled into the circular drive by the front doors, and everyone piled out.

The lodge's windows glowed, making the snow outside look like delicate flakes of gold. For being as large as it was, the building still retained a cozy, welcoming atmosphere.

The boys vied for her hands and led her inside to a room she hadn't been in yet. Two fireplaces flanked either side, while a wall of glass looked out over the lake and mountains. Overstuffed sofas and chairs were scattered throughout, with round tables and chairs filling in other spaces. Shelves held more games than she'd ever seen outside a box store, and several tellys were lined up, gaming consoles at the ready.

People filled most of the tables, and she recognized Hunter's family.

"Mackenzie, welcome," said a tall blond woman. It took Mack a moment to realize it was the one they called Frankie.

"Is this a family night? I don't want to intrude."

Frankie linked her arm through Mackenzie's. "One thing you learn very quickly here—the Sullivan family doesn't know a stranger. A few months ago, I came here for a work retreat with my company. Almost from the first day, they treated me and my son as family."

"Oh, is that how you met Wyatt?" Mackenzie glanced around the room until she spotted Wyatt holding little Johnny. They were talking, but when Wyatt looked over at Frankie, the love that shone there almost hurt her heart it was so powerful.

Frankie laughed. "Yes, that's when we met. Although the first day wasn't our best—it involved a pit of mud and the ruination of my brand-new pink shoes and favorite suit."

Mackenzie's eyes popped wide. "I think I need to hear this story."

"You're on. For now, let's get you settled in for game night."

Frankie led her to the bar—actually a hot cocoa bar, since the children were running around the room.

Suddenly, Hunter was next to her, stealing all the air from her lungs.

"Evenin', darlin'," he drawled, his voice deep and smooth, like the finest Scotch whiskey from home.

Her insides got all squishy, and she did the only thing she could think of. "Oh, stop." And shoved him with her elbow.

Frankie burst out laughing. "Oh, Lord, she's got your number, doesn't she, Hunter?" She slung an arm around Mackenzie's shoulder. "You're going to get along just great with us, sister."

Mackenzie kept quiet, sure she'd mangle whatever words she'd try to say. When she'd elbowed Hunter, she felt his rock-hard stomach, and immediately imagined perfectly chiseled abs…and much, much more.

Not that imagining would hurt anything, as long as

she didn't give him any sign she found him devastatingly attractive.

He already knew he was. And he wasn't above using it, wielding it like a sword.

He wasn't going to get away with it. Not with her. No way. No how.

So she'd continue to treat him like a pesky kid brother. To save herself.

"Wanna play a game?"

She looked up at him then, the half smile on his face, the slightly quirked eyebrow. His green eyes dropped just enough so she knew he was looking at her lips. *And just what kind of game do you have in mind?*

"Miss Mack. Miss Mack!"

She looked down at Eli and Maddy as they ran up to her.

"Come play Candyland with us," Maddy said.

Mackenzie grinned up at Hunter. "Seems I have an offer I can't refuse." She let the kids drag her to the other side of the room, and settled on the floor around a board game.

The rest of the children gathered around the board.

"You'll have to show me how to play. We didn't have this game at my house."

The kids all started talking. Mackenzie finally flung her hands up and laughed. "Wait a minute. Who is the best player?"

All the boys pointed to Maddy, and she preened under the attention.

"Okay, Miss Maddy, you teach me how to play."

Maddy got so involved in explaining the rules, her dark curls bobbed around her face, and she flung her arms as she talked.

Then they all determined placement, and an almost

bloodthirsty game commenced. It amazed Mackenzie how seriously they took it.

They played several rounds, and at one point, as she couldn't stop laughing, she looked across the room at Hunter and caught him staring at her.

His expression surprised her. It looked if he wanted to be with her at the kids' table instead of with his brothers at the poker table.

What was that about? She'd just raised her hand to beckon him over when the door opened and Carley walked in. She spotted Hunter, then walked as fast as her shiny blue high heels would let her. *High heels? At a ranch?*

Good thing Mackenzie hadn't encouraged him to join her and the kids.

Hunter groaned internally when Carley walked up to him at the poker table. He didn't want to hurt her feelings, but he'd had a change of heart about seeing her socially. His dad already discouraged the staff from fraternizing with guests. Though it had turned out all right for Nash and Wyatt.

Hunter had sworn off any serious relationships, wanting to focus on the boys. They had to come first.

"Hunter, I've been looking all over for you," Carley said, sliding her arm along his shoulders. She leaned into him, pressing her body against his back. "I'm bored," she whispered in his ear.

"I thought you were running lines tonight with your costar," he said, putting his cards down on the table.

"Come on, let's go do something," she said, the beginnings of a whine in her voice.

He stood up and led her to the lobby. "I'm real sorry, Carley. I'm tied up tonight."

"Tied up," she said, and stamped her foot. "You're playing cards in there with your brothers."

"Once a month we have family night."

She opened her mouth, and he knew she was about to give him an earful, so he held his hand up. "I know, it sounds ridiculous, but we actually conduct a lot of business on these nights." He grinned, hoping to placate her. "I'd ask you to join us, but we were just starting to talk about the plans for spring planting. And Luke has to go over the vaccination schedule for the cattle. You'd be totally bored listening to us drone on."

She huffed and folded her arms across her chest. "Oh, all right."

"Maybe another night soon?"

"We're doing the night scenes the next couple of nights, so I'll have to get back to you."

He nodded and pulled his wallet out. "Why don't you stop by the bar and get a bottle of wine you can share with your friends? It's on me." He handed her a card. "Enjoy."

As he watched her walk away, he breathed a sigh of relief. He should just tell her he wasn't interested, but he hated to hurt her feelings. *Man up, dumbass.*

He walked back in the game room and saw Kelsey had taken his spot at the table. Her cheeks glowed, and her eyes sparkled, and he was happy she was feeling better.

A rich laugh rang through the room, and he knew without looking it was Mackenzie. Her laugh always made him want to sit by her, be drawn into her world, make her laugh even more.

And it scared the hell out of him. Why did he feel this way? She wasn't the type to play around with. He knew that, dead to rights.

But they could be friends. Pals. Buddies.

Right?

Sure.

He watched her lean closer to the kids as they hung on her every word. Little Johnny had crept closer to her, and she put her arm around him as if it were second nature to her. Even Toby, who as the oldest cousin tended to be more standoffish, was sitting close, listening intently to her.

Hunter resisted as long as he could, till her laugh drew him over.

"When I was twelve, my dad's job took him to Aberdeenshire for a while, on the coast of Scotland. It's a beautiful place, and there are at least three hundred castles in the area."

"Castles? Real castles?" Maddy asked. "Like Prince Charming's castle?"

"Yes." Mackenzie nodded. "Some have been restored over the years, so you can visit and tour the inside, see the art and beautiful furnishings. Others are just ruins now—"

"What's a ruin?" Johnny asked.

Mackenzie smiled at him. "Ruins mean just parts of the outside are still standing. Like the rocks and stones used to build the castles of old. Those are the most fun to explore. You can tramp around inside them, playing lord and lady of the castle, and have tea parties and feasts. Or play Scottish warriors, come to rescue the fair princess being held in the castle."

"I wanna go to Scotland," Maddy said, beaming.

Hunter grinned to himself. Maddy would now be pestering Nash and Kelsey to take her to see a real castle in Scotland. Heck, Nash was so wrapped around her little finger, she'd probably convince him to *buy* her a castle.

"Dude, what're you doing?"

Kade's question beside him woke him from his reverie. "What?"

"You keep sniffing after Mackenzie, Carley will tear a strip off your hide."

"I'm not sniffing after anyone, Mackenzie or Carley," Hunter said. "Mackenzie tells great stories. You should listen to her sometime."

Kade looked at the group of kids around her as they all laughed. "Just be careful, especially since she's living with you."

"She's not *living* with me. She's using a room in my cabin since there wasn't anywhere else for her to go." He turned to Kade. "Hey, why can't she use your guest room?"

"I've got too much junk in there. The bed isn't even set up."

"So don't bug me. My hands were tied. Where'd you want her to stay—the barn?"

Kade raised his hands. "Just sayin'. You need to stop stringing Carley along. She's a guest, and not the type of person you want to piss off. She's a big name in Hollywood—in the news constantly. You piss her off, she tweets and lets the world know how bad she was treated at our ranch. Then reservations drop off, and we lose everything."

Hunter had to bite his tongue—he wanted to tell his brother to shut up, but Kade did have a point. However, Hunter had hated always being treated as the younger brother, the kid, who was constantly being told what to do.

"Just be careful," Kade said, and walked to the counter for a plate of food.

Hunter hesitated, then went ahead and walked over

to Mackenzie, still surrounded by the kids. She glanced up as he approached, and her smile dimmed just a bit. "Am I interrupting?"

Maddy popped up and flung herself at his legs. He caught her and lifted her up, kissed her cheek. "How's my favorite niece?"

She giggled. "I'm your only niece, silly."

"Well, this is true. But—"

She tapped his cheek. "I know, I know. I'm still your favorite niece."

"See?" he asked, tickling her until she laughed.

"Hey, everyone, can I have your attention, please?" Angus called out. The room quieted—as the family patriarch, he'd always commanded attention. "We're going to host a dinner dance for the cast and crew a few days from now in the southwest barn, since it's empty right now. Mrs. Green and her staff can use some extra help, so please sign up here." Hunter's dad held up a clipboard, then set it on the counter behind him.

"I volunteer Wyatt to make pies. Many, many pies," Hunter hollered above the voices.

Wyatt looked at him from across the room. "So, a couple for the guests, and five for you?"

"Make it six. You know I love me some pie." He set Maddy down, then reached a hand out to Mackenzie to help her off the floor.

She ignored his hand and rose fluidly on her own. "Can I help?"

"Nope. You're one of our guests." He took a step and leaned closer to her ear. "But you can save me a dance or two."

"I don't dance, but thanks for asking."

"Then share some pie with me."

"I, uh—" Her cheeks colored prettily, and she ran her hand through her hair.

"You haven't lived till you've tried Wyatt's pies."

"He bakes?"

"He bakes, cooks, grills a mean steak, shoes horses, mends fences and is a whiz with anything mechanical." He stepped close enough that he caught a whiff of her springlike scent. "But enough about my brother. He's already got a woman. Let's talk about me."

"Oh, go on with ye. You flirt with anyone who doesn't have a Y chromosome, I'll bet."

He affected a wounded look on his face. "Now, that hurts. Can I help it if women are drawn to me? I'm a catch, didn't you know? What woman wouldn't want to be around me?" His flirt-gene automatically kicked in and took him by surprise.

"Hunter, leave her alone." Kelsey joined them by the shelves of games.

"What'd I do?" he asked, enjoying the chase.

"You're pushing her into a corner. Literally." Kelsey pointed at her.

He looked at Mackenzie—she'd backed up so much she'd reached the corner where the two bookcases formed a V.

"We're just talking," he said.

"You're flirting, and she's wise to not want any of it," Frankie said as she moved next to Mackenzie.

He eyed all three women facing him. "Why do I get the feeling you're ganging up on me?"

"We have to stick together. There's entirely too much testosterone floating around this ranch," Kelsey said, and linked arms with Mackenzie, who then linked arms with Frankie.

"What's going on over here?" Bunny asked from behind him.

"We're joining forces to keep Hunter in line," Frankie said. "You in?"

Bunny scooted around him and linked arms with her daughter. "Can we have tea and cakes while we do it?"

"Sure thing, Mom," Kelsey said.

"Cake?" he asked, and rubbed his stomach.

Mackenzie laughed. "You're right. All he cares about is food and flirting."

He raised his hands in surrender. "All right, all right. I give up." He started walking away, then half-turned and caught Mackenzie watching him.

He liked teasing her, getting her riled up—her cheeks turned pink, and her fiery hair seemed to crackle with energy. She had become a part of his group, his family, even without meaning to. His boys sure adored her.

And he had to admit he'd gotten used to her being around.

But what would happen when she left?

Chapter 8

Mackenzie hung upside down from the hayloft rail in an empty barn and thought back to the night before with the Sullivans. Hunter had really flustered her. What was he after? Carley already had him wrapped around her fancy fingernails.

Bugger it. Surely he didn't expect her to be another one of his conquests. She kind of liked him—he seemed to be a good father, a good brother, from what she could tell.

But she couldn't figure out why he'd want to flirt with her. Carley was beautiful, smart, talented, famous. Mackenzie was just a no one from a foreign country, leaping from one job to the next…literally.

She pulled herself back upright and hopped up on the railing, carefully sliding one foot after the other.

The barn door creaked open, and she looked down to see one of the Triples walk in.

"Miss Mack? You in here?"

She looked closer, saw a hint of green shirt beneath the coat. "I'm up here, Eli," she called down to him.

He took off his miniature cowboy hat and looked up. "Whatcha doing up there?"

"Working out the next stunt to film. What are you doin', lad? Why aren't you in school?"

"School's out. Daddy's teaching us to be like him."

A flirt? "What do you mean?" She jumped off the railing, then climbed down the ladder.

"He's teaching us to be cowboys!" His grin was so big it stretched all across his cute little face.

"Well now, that should be fun." She smoothed a hand across his hair, but the cowlick sprang back up. It reminded her of her little brother Scotty's hair, though her brothers all had hair that was bright red and wildly curly.

Her own red hair was usually a bother to her in this job. Doubling for Carley on this movie was actually a decent gig—other than the dreaded fire scene. Mackenzie didn't have to wear a wig or dye her hair.

Eli looked up at the empty hayloft where she'd been practicing. "Show me how to do that, Miss Mack."

"It's awfully high. I don't think your dad would like it, do you?"

Eli looked down, digging the toe of his boot into the floorboard. "I guess not."

The door creaked open again. "Eli?" Hunter poked his head around the door. "Mackenzie. I didn't know you were in here."

"Just laying out the next stunts, then I'll go over them with the coordinator."

"Come on, Eli. Miss Mack is working. We need to get some of our own work in before dinner."

She watched as Hunter zipped Eli's coat back up and helped his son with his hat. Amazing Hunter could be responsible for three little lives, yet act like a kid himself. *Or teen boy*, she amended.

"We'll leave you to it. I think we'll be late tonight, so if you're hungry, you might want to eat at the lodge before you head home." He waved, and led Eli out of the barn, shutting the door tight against the cold.

Quiet descended again. Quiet led her thoughts to places she didn't want to go. Worry about her brothers, worry about her job, worry about why Hunter seemed to always flirt with her.

Sure, she was still gun-shy. Even after years of her mother warning her about men, she'd gotten her heart broken.

She rotated her neck, then shook herself out, from her arms and hands down to her legs and feet. "Relax," she muttered to herself. It was crucial she pay attention during stunt work.

The next few hours flew by as she worked through the routines. After a quick meeting with Brody to discuss the upcoming scenes, she was free to go.

On her way up the path, she heard children laughing, so she veered toward the sound. At the corral, she saw several Sullivan brothers, Kelsey and Frankie leaning against the railing, watching the action inside the corral.

She stopped next to Kelsey. "What's going on?"

"Hunter's teaching the boys how to rope steers," Kelsey said.

Mackenzie looked in the corral and saw several hay bales, with plastic steer heads stuck on the front, spaced around the area. "Aren't they a little young for that?"

Nash pulled his head back to answer her. "We all got started younger than them, so they're right on track."

She watched for a few more minutes as all three boys tried to lasso the fake steers, and Hunter would patiently correct their stance.

Then Mackenzie noticed Maddy sitting on the bottom railing, facing away from the corral, her little arms crossed over her chest.

"What's wrong, Maddy?" She squatted down on the ground in front of the little girl.

"Stupid boys. They said I can't be a cowboy 'cause I'm a girl." She sniffed.

"Well now, that's not very fair, is it?" Mackenzie stood up and whispered a question to Nash and Kelsey. Once she had their approval, she climbed up the fence and sat on the top rail.

She cupped her hands around her mouth. "Hey, Hunter," she called. She waited for him to look up. "Maddy wants to learn how to rope cows. Can she join you all?"

"Nah, she's a girl," Tripp hollered.

"She has dolls to play with," Cody chimed in. "She can make cookies and stuff for them."

The look on Hunter's face was pure shock. "Boys, that's not nice. Of course Maddy can try it if she wants to."

Mackenzie hopped down into the corral and pointed at Wyatt on the other side of the railing. "Your uncle bakes excellent pies, from what I hear. Does that make him girlie?"

The Triples all looked at Wyatt, and he crossed his arms, affecting a grimace on his face.

"Welllll…no, I guess not," Cody said, trailing his boot through the dirt.

"Remember what we talked about the other day when I taught you all how to tumble like Spider-Man? There's no such thing as just boy-only or girl-only things."

"Well, not some things." Hunter snickered as she reached his side.

She punched him lightly on the arm.

Hunter grinned. "Come on, guys, let her try. See if she likes it."

The boys all looked at each other in silence, then nodded as one, which kind of freaked Mackenzie out.

"Great," she said, and walked to the corral rail. "Maddy, you want to come learn how to use a lasso?"

Maddy looked up at her, grinning from ear to ear. She hopped up, then crawled between the rails.

Mackenzie took Maddy's hand in hers and walked with her to where Hunter stood.

"Have fun, Maddy," Mackenzie said and turned around to leave.

"Miss Mack, you show me," Maddy said, pulling on her sleeve.

"Don't you want your uncle Hunter to show you?"

Maddy shook her head, her black curls bouncing. "The Triples said you can do anything."

Hunter squatted down next to Maddy. "Miss Mackenzie can do anything in the movies. She didn't grow up on a ranch. Maybe she doesn't know how to do this."

"I can so do it." The words popped out before she could stop them.

Hunter turned his head up and squinted at her in the afternoon sunshine. He stood and took a step close. "You don't have to do this. There's a big difference between doing a stunt that can be fixed with movie magic, and real ranch work."

"You think I can't do it?"

He shrugged. "Just saying there's a difference between stunt work and real ranch work."

She slid a dirty look at him, and held her hand out for the rope. *I can do this. I learned how last year. Concentrate. And don't screw this up or I'll never live it down.*

Coiling the rope in her gloved hand, she made sure

the knot was right, then started twirling it out to the side, then over her head as it grew bigger. She focused on the steer closest to her and let the lasso fly. It sailed through the air, then landed exactly where she wanted it—around the steer's horns.

"Awesome. You got it—"

The words weren't even out of Hunter's mouth before she took off running toward the hay bale and flipped over it, and as she went, she grabbed the lasso off the horns. She kept running, twirled the lasso again and let it fly to a practice steer on the other side of the corral. The lasso landed true, right over the horns.

Proving her point kept her in action, lassoing and flipping, until she'd "captured" every steer in the corral.

Raucous applause finally made her look up. All of the family clapped and cheered. It was then that she noticed the assistant director standing on the other side, watching.

Hunter and his boys stood near the gate, and the look on his face was all she'd hoped for. At least it had shut him up about real versus stunt work.

"Hey, bro. I'd say she's the clear winner here." Nash stuck his arm through the railing and punched his shoulder.

"So what do ye say now, cowboy?" she asked Hunter as she walked toward him.

"Well, you're trained to do that kind of stuff. Flips aren't part of ranch work."

"I don't do things halfway. What I just did can't be edited into a movie and have it look right. That is real work. Hard work." She stopped, close enough to poke his chest.

He held his hands up and stepped back.

"You think I can't do what you do on a ranch?" She stepped forward again, crowding him against the rail his brothers leaned on.

"I'm just saying this is a real working ranch, real life. We ride, shoot, rope for a living—not do flips and stunts."

"Why don't you put your pennies where your pie-hole is?" She taunted him before she could stop herself.

He opened his mouth, but nothing came out.

"What's wrong? Chicken?" Kade added his own punch to Hunter's shoulder.

Hunter took his glove off and stuck his hand out. "You got a deal."

His hand enveloped hers. They locked eyes, and she wasn't sure if he was really angry or not.

"When and where, cowboy?" she asked.

"Tomorrow morning," he said. "That'll give us time to get chores done and set up."

She glanced out the other side of the corral and saw the director talking with the AD. *Criminy, I should have checked with Tom first.* Before she could move, Tom raised his head, looked at her, then Hunter, and nodded.

"Aye, that works. See you then." She waved at the boys, then ducked under the railing.

Once again she'd let her temper overrule her mouth.

She'd grown up with a father who taught her that she could do anything and everything. She'd never wanted to take ballet lessons. Her favorite had been gymnastics classes, which had served her well in her career.

And she'd wanted to be outside, working on their farm, with the horses, and learning from her dad. When he was gone, her brothers goaded her into making sure she could do it all, be the best she could be.

Chapter 9

Hunter stood in the open doorway of the barn and finished his coffee as he looked out over the once again snowy field, thanks to the snowfall during the night. Deer prints trailed from one side of the barn and out into a copse of bare trees. Several red cardinals swooped through the air, then perched in a tree. They reminded him of Christmas decorations on an evergreen, waiting for the lights to be turned on.

Some of the ranch hands had set up the skeet-shooting stations for the contest between him and Mackenzie in an open field, safe from buildings, stock and guests. His family—and some of the ranch employees who were off for the day—had already lined the back of the area. He looked closer and saw people he didn't recognize. Were they from the film crew?

He rolled his eyes. *Great.* He couldn't believe he'd let himself be talked into this, and that a lot more than his family would be watching.

This was a matter of pride now. And the proverbial yanking on the pigtails of a girl he liked. For the fifteenth—okay, maybe the fiftieth time—he wondered why he was attracted to Mackenzie. *Prickly, stubborn tomboy.*

But then there'd be something in her eyes, something that beckoned to him, made him want to crawl inside her head and see how she viewed the world, find out what secrets she held so close.

She'd been asleep the night before by the time he and the boys had gotten home, so they hadn't been able to talk. He wondered if maybe she'd planned it that way.

Or maybe she was just exhausted. She did work hard. He'd caught a glimpse—*okay, spied on her*—doing some of her stunt work the other day. She definitely had talent, he had to give her that. Her job was all about being physical.

She was one tough lady—at least on the outside. Doing stunts had to hurt some of the time.

Sure, he'd been kicked by cows and horses, thrown several times, even fallen out of the hayloft a time or two. But those weren't intentional injuries. Granted there were safety precautions for stunt doubles, but it still blew his mind anyone—much less a pretty woman—would want to do that for a living.

The sound of footsteps crunching on the snow broke the morning silence. Mackenzie strode toward the barn where he stood. Her hair gleamed like copper threads in the early-morning sun.

She raised her head, and he knew the second she spotted him. The slightest hitch to her gait told him he'd gotten under her skin. Good. Maybe then she'd know how he felt.

But maybe she wasn't attracted to him at all. And wouldn't that be a shame.

"Top o' the mornin' to ye, lassie," he said, and tipped his cowboy hat at her.

"That's Irish," she scoffed back.

"Then how do you say *good morning* in Scottish?"

She smiled at him, teeth bared. *"Madainn mhath."*

"Okay, then, what you said." He sipped the last of his coffee, swallowed. "Sleep okay?"

"Fine," she said. "Like a kitten with a belly full of milk."

"Not worried about today?"

"Why would I be?" She began to wrestle her thick curls into a single braid down her back. "Are you?"

His tongue felt thick as he watched her hands work. Fingers twitching, he almost had to fight to keep his hands away from that hair. He wanted to dive into it, the whole unruly, gloriously bright mass of it. "Am I what?"

"Are you worried about the challenge?"

He slowly shook his head. Wondered why they were having this stupid conversation when they could be using their mouths—lips and tongues—in a much better way. Like kissing.

Her skin was a pale cream, with freckles dotted across her nose. His eyes drifted just a bit lower, to lips the color of a ripe, juicy berry.

He had to snap out of this, or next thing he knew he'd be spouting poetry or something.

His dad walked up to them and clapped him on the back. "Morning, you two. Ready to start?"

Hunter looked at her. "Not too late to back out now, you know."

She straightened up tall. "Not on your life. Lead on, cowboy."

He gestured for her to precede him, and then followed her to the skeet setup.

Voices faded to an indistinct murmur in the background. The morning sun was warming the day up—at least as warm as late March could be in Montana.

They'd haggled on the details the day before, deciding to break it up into a couple of days so as not to take too much time away from filming or regular ranch work.

While he and Mackenzie were being outfitted with safety equipment, vests and shotguns, his dad flipped the coin that decided Hunter would be first. He stepped up and got in position, then shouted, "Pull!"

With a snap, the first clay pigeon sped out of the station. He aimed and pulled the trigger, blew it out of the air. A second crossed his line of sight, and he barely clipped it. It kept sailing through the air.

Mackenzie stepped up for her turn and lifted the shotgun into place. One quick shot, and the clay broke. Another shot, and the lower clay exploded into a million pieces.

They continued taking turns, advancing to each station.

By the time they reached the eighth station, he and Mackenzie were tied. He stepped up and shouted, "Pull."

He aimed and squeezed the trigger, and the clay pigeon exploded. Shot again, and his last one exploded, too.

Cheering erupted from the onlookers, drowning out the echo of gunshots, and he turned around. His boys were jumping up and down, waving their hats. They looked like it was Christmas morning and Santa had brought them everything on their lists.

He waved at them, bowed to the onlookers, then glanced up at Mackenzie. From his angle, she seemed to be watching his boys, but the wistful expression on her face had him worried.

Closing the distance between them, he leaned toward her ear. "You okay?"

She nodded once. "Aye."

"You sure?"

She half smiled. "Missing my brothers, wishing the little heathens were here to watch me smoke you."

He laughed. "You mean to see me take home the trophy?"

Rolling her eyes, she turned on her heel and got in position. But she swiveled her head once more toward their audience, then back again, and shouted the command to release the clay pigeons.

Her shot rang true and clear through the cold air, and the pigeon exploded. She swung the gun in an arc for the next clay, pulled the trigger and just clipped the clay as it sailed by.

Passing the shotgun off to the handler, she took off her safety glasses and earbuds. She walked toward Hunter, ungloved hand outstretched. "Well done, boyo."

He pulled off his own glove, clasped her hand in his. Held it when she went to pull away. "I'd call that a draw. You'll get it tomorrow."

"You bet your bahookie I will." She walked away, stopped to talk to one of the crew members who hailed her.

Hunter watched as the other man flung an arm out toward the skeet-shooting station, then looked at him. Mackenzie shook her head. She glanced at him, and waved when she saw him watching her. What was that about?

He stared back at the skeet stations now, wondering if she'd intentionally missed the last shot so he'd win.

No way. One thing he surmised about Mackenzie— she was not a fake. She'd never intentionally lose to anyone—especially him.

* * *

Mackenzie opened the door to Hunter's cabin and heard a loud booming noise. She pulled off her winter boots and hurried inside, relaxed when she realized music had been turned to blasting level. The song finished, and the lead-in for the next began with a steady drum beat. As she walked toward the kitchen, she noticed the Triples were sitting on bar stools at the island, and Hunter was stirring something on the stove.

The beat of the music started picking up, and Hunter was moving in time to the beat. His hips moved side to side, then his head started moving back and forth, keeping the beat as it accelerated.

The lyrics started, and he added his shoulders to the mix, then he whirled to face the boys, swinging the wooden spoon up to use as a microphone. A glob of whatever he'd been stirring splatted in front of Cody on the counter.

The boys all looked at each other as if their dad had suddenly gone stark bonkers. Hunter kept singing and dancing in the kitchen, and the boys started laughing.

She recognized the song was "Footloose." Not a favorite film, but she'd loved it when the young actress jumped from one car to the other as they raced down the highway. For the first time, she wondered if she'd had an itch for stunt work all those years ago.

The longer she watched, the more she admired this grown man, with triplets no less, as he danced and sang around the kitchen. He had good moves, too, keeping in time to the energetic music. He stopped at the stove, hips continuing to move, and stirred whatever he was cooking. Executing a twirl, he swung the spoon back up and around, flinging more food.

She leaned against the wall and folded her arms, trying to keep quiet. But his good mood was contagious, and she started laughing.

By now the boys were hooting with laughter, looking like they were having the best time, and she didn't want to intrude. She was tempted to go to her room and leave them to have fun, but Hunter executed some fancy dance moves, and she couldn't look away. His flannel shirt hung loose and unbuttoned over his T-shirt, denim jeans worn white in some areas and butter soft cowboy boots.

He twirled around, arms swinging with abandon, and that was when saw her. He froze for a split second, and she was afraid he'd stop. Then he shimmied over to her and held his hand out. She protested, but he grabbed her hand and pulled her all the way into the kitchen, to the space between the island and table.

He twirled her outward, then pulled her in again. As he guided her in a loose swing dance, she picked up the beat and matched his timing.

They twirled and swung and bopped around the kitchen, and she was near breathless from laughing and dancing. At long last, the song started winding down, but Hunter swung around and picked up a remote off the counter, aimed it toward a stereo and started it again.

This time he lifted each of his sons off their stools and they began to dance, too. At least, she thought it was dancing. She reached for one hand flinging through the air and twirled one of the triplets—Eli—into a swing dance. He beamed up at her, looking so happy she could just eat him up.

Tripp bopped past her, and she grabbed his hand, twirled him around and the three of them danced in a crazy circle. Their circle grew as Cody cut in, then Hunter.

She had to admit this was the most fun she'd had in…well, ages.

The song wound down again, and this time Hunter let it stop. She plopped down in one of the kitchen chairs, trying to gulp in air and stop laughing.

"I thought you told me before you can't dance?" Hunter asked in a bland tone as he walked to the stove and stirred again, sending her off into another round of laughter.

She wiped her eyes. "I didn't say I can't dance, just that I don't. I haven't danced in forever. I must admit that was a cracking good time. You—all of you—are grand dancers. I'm fair puggled."

"You're what?" asked Cody. "A pug dog?"

"It's a Scot's way of sayin' they're plum worn out."

"Then I'm fair puggled, too," Hunter said from the stove. "And you're just in time for dinner."

"You don't need to feed me again," she said. "I don't want to intrude."

He swung his head around. "Boys, is she intruding?"

"No!" their voices chorused and rose, each trying to be the loudest.

"See?"

She got out of the chair. "Then let me help, at least."

"It's all done." He carried the pot to the table and set it on a trivet, then brought a platter heaped with hot dogs in buns. A bag of chips followed, and he pulled her chair out for her with a flourish. He affected a terrible British accent and said, "Dinner is served."

She sat down, and he pulled out the chair next to her. The boys shoved their way onto the bench seat in the alcove.

Hunter picked up a bowl and held a big ladle over the pot. "Chili in a bowl or on hot dogs?"

"I've eaten chili before, and hot dogs. But I've never had chili on a hot dog." She wasn't quite sure it sounded very appealing.

"No way!" Cody said. "It's our favorite food!"

Hunter nodded. "It's true. When I let them choose what they want for dinner, that's the one thing they pick every time."

"Well, if you all love it so much, I guess I'll have to take your word that it's good and give it a try."

Hunter put two hot dogs on a plate, then ladled chili across each one and passed the meal to her. "Ladies first."

She stared down at the food, wondering if she was supposed to pick one of the buns up like a normal hot dog or cut it with a fork so she didn't drip chili all over.

He finished serving up food for the boys, then dished up his own plate.

She watched the boys pick up their hot dogs and eat them with so much gusto she couldn't wait to try hers. Picking it up, a chili bean fell off, followed by a dribble of liquid. She licked the bun to catch the next drip, then noticed Hunter watching her.

"Wha'?" she mumbled.

He grinned and took a bite of his own.

She bit into the hot dog and chili combo, and it surprised her how good it was. The more she ate, the more she liked it.

"You got some chili on your mouth," Hunter said.

She licked one side, then the other. "Did I get it?"

He pointed just below his own lip.

She licked again, then grabbed her napkin. "Now?"

He raised his hand and used his thumb to wipe it off.

It was innocent, she knew it, but it felt so intimate. Sitting in his kitchen in her stockinged feet, the snow outside cocooning them in the warm alcove. She inhaled, then choked on air, and grabbed her glass of water and took a sip.

Even looking down, she felt his eyes on her, and she refused to meet his gaze. Instead she looked at the Triples. "Well, boys, that's my new favorite meal, too."

"Yay!" they shouted.

"What's for dessert, Daddy?" Tripp asked.

"You just gorged on chili dogs and potato chips. How can you still be hungry?" Hunter asked.

"If they're anything like my brothers, they saved a spot for dessert way down in their toes. Am I right, boys?" she said.

"I even got room left in my knees," Cody said.

"Mrs. Green did send some brownies," Hunter said. "Clear your plates and we'll have some."

She pushed her chair back, but he rested a hand on her shoulder, then squeezed lightly. "Stay. We'll get it."

Sitting back, she scolded herself for reading anything into his gesture.

Eli and Tripp each brought a short stack of bowls to the table and set them down. Cody followed, bringing forks and spoons. They took their seats again, this time with a minimum of pushing and shoving.

Hunter set a cake pan and a bowl in the middle of the table.

Brownies. Specifically iced brownies. She peeked in the blue ceramic bowl. "You put ice cream on brownies?"

He looked at her. "You don't?"

"I've not thought of it."

"Then you're in for a treat. Mrs. Green's homemade vanilla bean ice cream."

She patted her stomach. "I better not. If I keep eating like this, I'll not be able to do my stunts tomorrow."

"You'll regret saying that in a minute." He grabbed her spoon and dipped it in the bowl of ice cream, scooped up a taste. "Open up." He held out the spoon, and she opened her mouth.

Cold coated her tongue, and then the flavor hit her taste buds. "I wouldn't want Mrs. Green to think I'm rude. But just a wee bit, please."

Hunter sliced a brownie for her, topped it with ice cream and set the bowl in front of her. Then repeated the steps for each one of them.

"Daaaaddy, you forgot the best part," Cody said.

"You're right, pal. Go get it."

Cody jumped up from the end of the bench and raced to the refrigerator, then came back with a can of whipped cream. He set it down in front of her, then scooted back onto the bench seat.

"You add that, too?" she asked.

Hunter just slid his eyes to her, the *duh* implied.

She held her hands up in surrender. "Okay, just asking." She picked up the can, gave it a good shake and took the top off. "Who wants some?"

All three boys shot their hands up in the air.

"Okay, hold your bowls up for me." She leaned forward and squirted some in Cody's bowl first.

He looked from her to the bowl, then back again at her.

"What, not enough?"

"Nope."

She leaned forward and squirted more in the bowl, then tilted it up and coated his fingers. "Oops, I missed the bowl!" she said, faking embarrassment. She moved the can to Eli's bowl, topped it and squirted some on the back of his hand.

"Me next!" Tripp said.

"Are you suuure you want some?" she asked.

He nodded so vigorously she was afraid he'd fall off the bench.

"Yes, sir." She topped his brownie and ice cream, then kept squirting whipped topping up to his wrist.

The boys all hooted, licking their hands off.

She turned to Hunter. "How much do you want?" she asked, then felt herself go red when he looked at her with so much heat she was surprised the ice cream didn't melt on the spot.

"All of it," he murmured beneath the boys' chatter.

"Mustn't be greedy," she said just loud enough for him to hear her.

"I can handle it. Can you?"

Chapter 10

The cheerful kitchen faded around her as Mackenzie stared into Hunter's eyes. She knew they weren't talking about dessert. The longer she looked at him, the hotter she got. So not what she needed. Hardly even thinking about it, she lifted the can and squirted a dollop on his nose.

He looked as surprised as she felt at doing it. Then he smiled, slow, and scooped it off.

She plopped back into her chair and grabbed her bowl, shoveling in a bite of ice cream. As soon as they were through with dessert, she'd scoot off to her room and lock the door, throw herself into work or making more necklaces. Anything to keep her mind occupied.

The boys hopped up and asked to be excused. She jumped up as fast as they had, and began clearing the table. Taking a load to the sink to be rinsed, she turned around and almost slammed into Hunter. She kept her eyes focused on his chest, not risking a look up at him. Not when she knew her interest in him would be shining there.

For several long heartbeats, he didn't move or speak.

The heat from his body was welcome, considering she was frozen inside and out. Inhaling, she caught the scent of his aftershave, the one she'd wanted to snuggle into the other morning when they'd camped in the fort.

Then he raised his hand and used one finger to lift her chin up. He wasn't smiling, and his eyes looked deep inside her.

She couldn't force herself to look away.

"You don't need to do that."

"Do what?" she asked, hating that her voice had gone breathy.

"Clear the table. Avoid me. Pick one."

"I'll be leaving soon. I can't do this," she said, and pushed away from him.

He caught her wrist and held it lightly. "Do what?"

"I—" she began, then stopped when one of the boys thundered into the kitchen.

"Miss Mack, will you read to us?"

"I'll read to you, boys," Hunter said, and he set a bowl by the sink.

"Naw, we want Miss Mack. She has a pretty voice. Puhleeze?"

"Sure, Eli. Show me which book you want." She took Eli's hand and walked out of the kitchen.

Almost half an hour later, she'd read two books to them, then was halfway through the third when she heard sniffles. She looked at each boy—Cody and Tripp were asleep, but Eli was curled in the corner of the couch now, crying.

She set the book down and scooted over to him. "What's wrong, lad? Did I read it wrong?"

"What happened?" Hunter hurried into the room, a dish towel draped over his shoulder.

"I dinna ken. I was reading this book to them." She held it up.

A pained look crossed his face, and he rubbed a hand down his mouth. He leaned closer to her. "That's the book his mom used to always read to him. Their little ritual."

"Oh, no. He handed it to me after the last book. I'm so sorry," she whispered, her throat tight.

"You didn't know." He lifted Eli up into a hug. "Come on, pal, let's go upstairs." He carried Eli up the steps and disappeared from her view.

She wavered, not sure if she should wake the other two so they could head to bed or keep them with her so Hunter could talk to Eli.

"Mommy?" Cody sat up, rubbing his eyes.

She swiped her eyes so they wouldn't see her sad for them. "It's me, Mackenzie. Your da took Eli upstairs. Do you want to go with them or stay here?"

Cody got up and yanked on his brother's arm, and they both ran upstairs.

She'd made the right decision. Remembering her little brothers after their mother died, they'd always wanted her, not a friend or a babysitter.

She busied herself in the kitchen, finishing up the dishes and cleaning stray spots of chili that had been flung around during the dance session. Once the kitchen sparkled, she walked back into the living room. Along the way, she put the books away, picked up toys and other little boy stuff, and turned off lights.

Hunter's thick denim jacket was slung over the back of a chair by the windows, and she picked it up. The garment was old and well-worn, and she wanted to bundle herself in its softness. She folded it into her arms, breathed in his scent, content to do so now that it wasn't him in person. Leaning against the window frame in the shadows, she looked out, watching big flakes fall gently to the ground.

Yawning, she turned around and saw Hunter had come downstairs and was sitting on the sofa. He held his head in his hands, looking so defeated and broken it frightened her. She set the jacket down and crossed the room, then sat down at the end of the sofa. "Is Eli okay?"

He jerked his head up. "I didn't know you were still up." Pain laced his words.

"I wanted to see if the wee one was all right."

He rubbed his eyes, the low light from the dying fire casting shadows across his chiseled face. "At times they all seem fine. Then suddenly, boom. They just break down."

"That will happen for a long time to come, I'm afraid."

He grimaced. "Great. I'd hoped you'd say they would be fine."

"They *will* be fine. They've got you, and they've got their aunts and uncles, cousins, grandparents, who would all walk to the ends of the earth for you and your boys."

He looked at her, eyebrows raised.

"What? You think I haven't noticed how your family is? I envy you that. For me, it's just my brothers. Don't get me wrong, I adore them, and we're close. But to have such an extended family is a treasure."

"It wasn't always that way. Nash and Wyatt both left. Couldn't handle Dad and the arguments, his expectations, anymore." His voice cracked, and he rubbed his chin. "Our mom died not long after I was born. I never knew her. Nash was ten, so he tried to keep us going. Dad had it rough. Suddenly alone, and with five boys. As we grew older, we all had clashes with him. Then they left. And I don't know why I just told you all of that."

"Sometimes it helps to talk to someone you don't know well."

"It was hard, losing Yvette. I cared about her, but we just couldn't make it together. I can't imagine what my dad went through after Mom died. Bunny really mellowed him. They're great together. They've all helped me with the boys. I just worry I'm not enough. That they need more than what I can give them."

Shocked, she scooted closer to him, laid her hand on his back.

His shoulders hunched. "I used to get them on weekends and holidays. Now I'm all they've got. I need a full-time dad's playbook."

"Give yourself some credit. You're their father, and you adore them. And they absolutely love you. I've seen the way they watch you, try to emulate you." She felt his muscles shift beneath her hand as he shrugged.

"What if they're too broken?"

"They're going through a very difficult time, but you're there for them day in and day out. I know how hard it is to raise children, and believe me, you're doing a great job. When you took Eli upstairs, did he talk to you?"

He nodded.

"That right there is a good thing. If he had shut you out, there might be a problem. But you're there for them and they know it. You'll help them through every day, every night. Keep the communication open with the boys, keep doing what you're doing."

His body turned toward her, leaned in just a bit.

She swallowed hard. "Do you know what I saw when I walked in tonight? I saw a man taking time out of his day, after working all day to boot, and—" she smiled in the near dark "—after *almost* winning a shooting competition to make his boys laugh. The men I know would have just wanted to get dinner cooked, get the kids ready for bed, then settle by themselves in front of the telly. But you didn't do that. You never do that. You give them your time, your attention and your love. That's a treasure they'll always have as they grow up, as they move on to their own lives and families."

His eyes seemed to glow and reflect the fire as he stared at her. She hoped she'd reached him, given him some peace.

He leaned forward enough to touch his forehead to hers. "Thank you," he whispered, his breath on her lips. "I struggle every damn day not knowing what to do, how to handle things for them. Worrying I'll do something wrong and screw them up forever."

"Just keep loving them as you are." She started to pull away, but he brushed her cheek, held her in place.

"You're one hell of a woman, Mackenzie Campbell. I'm really glad you came to our ranch."

He drew back and she couldn't look away. Pain, relief, maybe even desire, flickered across his face.

Closing the distance, keeping his eyes on her, he finally pressed his lips to her. His mouth slid across hers in a joining so sweet she ached. His fingers slid down her cheek to her neck, and she wondered if he could feel her pulse galloping, wild and free.

He stilled, just for a moment, and just as she started to pull back, he slanted his mouth over hers and took the kiss deep. So deep she didn't think—no, she knew—she'd never been kissed this way before.

The few others she'd kissed had been mere boys. This was a man. Oh, blessed Saint Margaret, was he ever a man.

She felt his kisses all through her body, all the way to her toes. Her heart just about thumped out of her chest, and she wanted to scream, laugh and cry all at once. The riot of emotions scared her.

He shifted, pulled her closer, wrapped his arms around her. She felt protected, desired, cherished.

Wanton.

They were just kissing, but it was kissing like she'd never done before, or even dreamed of.

Chemistry. She'd heard about people who had chemistry, and never really understood it.

Now she did.

Kissing him was like coming home to a warm fire, then having the house explode around you while you had a cracking good time.

She wanted to touch him as he touched her. Suddenly realized she could, since he'd initiated the kiss. Tentatively she brought her hand up to his arm, and felt his biceps shift. She slid her hand up higher, to his shoulder, then slipped her fingers beneath his shirt collar to the bare skin of his neck.

He groaned, and the sound rumbled through her all the way down to her girlie bits.

A log shifted and crackled, the sound like a gunshot in the quiet room. They pulled apart at the same time. Stared at each other.

Her heart thudded, once…twice. And she jumped up, then raced to her room like the Loch Ness Monster really was after her.

But she couldn't outrun her feelings.

Chapter 11

Mackenzie pulled an arrow out of the quiver and nocked it in place. Pulling the bowstring back, she let her deltoid muscles do all the work. She pulled past the resistance, all the way to her anchor point, her finger lightly touching the corner of her mouth.

They were back in the same area as the day before. This time there were more people watching, their voices blending in the cool breeze as it shivered through the tree branches.

Aiming, she blew out a breath, forcing herself to relax. *Focus on the target.* She released the bowstring, and the arrow raced through the air. She squinted in the weak morning light. The arrow hit the target just a hair off the center mark.

Bloody hell.

She'd tried all night to get Hunter out of her head. Squeezing her eyes closed, she envisioned locking him in a box.

She nocked the next arrow in place, pulled, released. This time it hit true center.

The third arrow hit dead center also.

She stepped off her mark and turned around.

Hunter was watching her. *What is goin' through that head o' his?* Their kiss the night before had rocked her world. Had he been affected just as much?

She nodded at him, then hurried out of the way so he could take his turn.

They'd agreed to shoot three arrows each, in five rounds.

Hunter stood ready, drew his bowstring back and let the arrow fly. She followed the arrow's trajectory, and could tell it would hit the center.

The next arrow also hit center, but the third landed just out of the red target.

A squeal echoed behind her, and she saw Carley run up to Hunter as he left the mark. She stood on tiptoe, but he stepped back before she could kiss his cheek.

Interesting. As she walked to the position, Hunter backed away, but Carley waited for her.

"Win or lose, you're not his type," Carley said.

"Who says I bloody hell want him?" Mackenzie snapped.

"I'm just trying to help you so you don't get hurt," Carley huffed.

Mackenzie watched her walk away, swinging her arse. Glancing at the crowd, she saw quite a few men watch as she pranced by them. Snorting in disgust, she took her place.

Her heart raced, and she knew she had to calm down, but Carley's remarks had made her so angry.

She nocked an arrow, then something made her glance behind her. Hunter watched her, but she could see Carley behind him, laughing with Bryant, her co-star, and pointing her way.

Well, she'd show them.

She went inside herself, tuned everything out so all she could hear was her own breath, her own heart beating. Just her and the bow.

Drawing the bowstring back, she released the arrow, then immediately pulled another arrow out, nocked, let it fly. She went beyond the three arrows and sent all six flying, one after the other.

Every one of them hit the center and formed a tight circle.

Dead silence met her as she lowered the bow. Then applause and cheers filled the cold morning air. She glanced at Hunter—he stood slack-jawed, eyebrows raised.

When would she learn to control her temper?

Hunter walked toward her, held his hand out. "That was—"

Heat and embarrassment crawled up her chest, inched up her neck. "Not sporting."

"Are you kidding? That was awesome. Amazing. Pure talent."

"Really? You're not angry?"

"Why would I be angry? Not everyone could do something like that, even practicing for years on end."

His praise filled her up. "So you admit that I do real work, not fake Hollywood stuff?"

"Of course."

Now she was confused. "Then why have the competition?"

"I like watching you in action. You're a natural at riding, shooting and archery." He grinned at her.

She narrowed her eyes at him, wished she had her granny's old cast iron skillet in hand to bop him over the head. "That's no' verra nice of ye."

"Your face is so alive when you're ticked off. Your red hair practically crackles with energy. And I wanted to see what you could do with a shotgun and a bow and arrow. You've got a lot of innate talent. You do anything you set your mind to, don't you?"

She was at a complete loss. He'd just admitted to teasing her on purpose, then he'd gone and complimented her on things she'd worked hard at learning, worked hard at being the best she could be.

His interest had become pretty clear. She hated that she still had trouble trusting men who showed their interest in her.

It wasn't a bet with his brothers, was it? She'd already had her heart broken once by a bet. She had to protect herself.

What would happen when it was time for her to go? That was the billion-dollar question that kept her tossing and turning at night.

Hunter took his hat off as he walked inside the lodge.

"There you are, darling!" Carley called from the staircase.

Inwardly, he groaned. He needed to let her down easy. He'd known from the beginning this was just a flirtation, on both their parts. He dreaded that Carley might be wanting more now. Mackenzie had become too important to him.

He smiled at Carley as she crossed the lobby to his side. "Hey."

"I need to talk to you," she said. "Could we go somewhere private? It won't take long."

"Sure. I need to talk to you, too." He led her to one of the smaller meeting rooms off the lobby, then closed the door behind them. "Have a seat."

"I have to get back to the set in a few minutes. I'm so glad we met up," she said, sliding her hand up his arm.

"Look, Carley. I can't see you—"

"I'm getting back together with Bryant," she said in a rush, interrupting him.

"Excuse me?"

"Seeing me with you made Bryant super jealous, and he begged me to come back to him."

"Then I'm happy for you," he said.

"I have to run," she said, and opened the door. As she stepped out in the lobby, she blew him a kiss. "Ciao!"

That was easy. Here he'd worried that he would hurt her by admitting he hadn't really been interested in her at all. Now he didn't have to.

Now he was free. It was what he wanted, right?

But his thoughts drifted to the kiss with Mackenzie the night before. He'd just wanted to thank her for making him feel like he wasn't a failure when it came to being a dad. An innocent kiss was what he'd intended.

Then he'd touched her lips, and he felt like he'd come home. That he was kissing the woman for him. He'd never felt like that with Yvette. Yeah, they'd loved each other, but they'd been so young, it felt more like playing house.

Mackenzie was a hell of a woman. When he'd first met her, he thought she was prickly, a tumbleweed. But she had more depth than he'd ever imagined. Kind, sweet, patient with his sons, caring, funny as hell, brave, talented—yes, still prickly. He'd had fun teasing her, getting her riled up—that was when she came alive.

Now he knew she also came alive when he kissed her. And she'd touched a part of him he thought had died a long time ago.

Chapter 12

Mackenzie knocked on the door to Frankie's cabin. She'd been invited to tea by the women of the Sullivan family. She liked them, wanted to get to know them better, but the invitation had surprised her. She wasn't really even a guest at the ranch—she was here to work.

She really didn't have any close female friends. Having grown up with brothers, and now working in the stunt field, she was mostly around men. She ran a hand over her hair again, making sure it hadn't sprung up all over her head, and hoped she wouldn't do anything to embarrass herself at tea.

The door opened. "Hi, Mackenzie. Come on in," Frankie said. "Kelsey and Bunny are already here." She led the way into a living room that opened onto a dream kitchen. Like Hunter's cabin, this one had a wall of glass that looked out on a spectacular view.

"Hello," Mackenzie said, and gave a little wave.

Kelsey waved from the sofa. "Pardon me for not getting up." She rubbed her pregnant belly. "This one is finally settled down, and I'm afraid to move."

Bunny hopped up and gave Mackenzie a quick hug. "Welcome to tea. We're so glad you could join us."

"Thank you for having me." She pulled three small packages out of her tote bag. "I want to give you each a little something for being so kind to me." She handed a small silk bag to each of the three women.

Frankie opened her bag and pulled out the necklace. "This is beautiful! You don't need to give us anything." She sifted the beads through her fingers. "Blue is my favorite color. Thank you."

Bunny held up the necklace made of all shades of pink and purple. "Exquisite. Thank you, my dear."

Kelsey opened her bag and pulled out the necklace she'd used green and brown beads for. "Did you make these necklaces? They're gorgeous. Thank you!"

"I did. I'm glad you like them. I find myself missing home often, and working with beads that remind me of the heather and thistle, the Highlands and the sea helps combat the homesickness." What she didn't tell them was a kind volunteer had gotten her involved in making jewelry when she was laid up for so long in hospital. It had saved her sanity many times by keeping her hands busy.

"How do you have time for this with such an active job?"

"I do it between takes, or at nights when I'm on the road with the film crew."

"Do you sell them?" Bunny asked.

"No, I usually donate them to a charity back home to sell at their fund-raisers."

"You could start a business. You're very talented," Frankie said. "If you ever decide to do it, call me. I'll help you navigate the start-up. I know Hunter would help you with marketing."

"Thank you," she said. Wow. These women were so kind with a virtual stranger.

Bunny gave her another quick hug. "Have a seat right over here," she said, and led her to one of the side chairs.

"Tea is ready," Frankie said, and wheeled a cart over.

Mackenzie's eyes just about popped out. "Are there more people coming?"

"No, why?" Frankie asked. Then looked at the cart laden with tea sandwiches and sweets. "Oh. Wyatt's been experimenting with desserts for the dance tonight, and you all get to be the guinea pigs—I mean taste testers!" She laughed.

Kelsey groaned. "Considering I want one of everything on that cart, *pig* is the appropriate term. I don't think I ever got this hungry when I was pregnant with Maddy."

"You weren't, pumpkin. That's why I think you're going to have a boy," Bunny said, and patted her daughter's hand.

Kelsey sighed, a dreamy smile on her face. "Nash would love that, wouldn't he?"

Frankie handed Mackenzie a plate. "Please, help yourself."

She got up and stepped to the cart. "Kelsey, what would you like?" Mackenzie asked. "You should get first choice."

Kelsey waved her hand. "Just take what you want and when everyone is served, Frankie can park that cart right next to me. I'll plow through everything that's left." She grinned sheepishly as everyone laughed.

Mackenzie chose a few treats, then sat down with a plate and a cup of tea.

"So, Mackenzie," Bunny said, and took a sip of tea, then swallowed. "What do you think of Hunter?"

The bite of cookie Mackenzie had just taken went down the wrong way, and she coughed, then gulped her tea. "Excuse me?"

"Hunter. The youngest Sullivan brother. The one you're living with right now," Bunny said, waving her fork in the air.

"Um, I'm not exactly living with him. I'm staying in an empty room in his cabin."

"That's semantics. What do you think of him?"

"He's a very good father," she said.

"And?" Frankie leaned forward.

"Good with a shotgun."

"What else?" This from Kelsey.

What did they expect her to say? That he was a bloody good kisser, and she'd started having fantasies about him? Mackenzie sipped her tea, leaned forward and added a dollop more milk. "He rides well?"

"Oh, for heaven's sake. Do you *like* him?" Bunny huffed.

"He seems to be a nice man. I mean, he took a stranger who needed a place to stay into his home." Eyeing the frustration on the faces of the other three women, she started having fun.

"I think you know what we mean, Mackenzie," Kelsey said, her voice mild.

"Oh?" she asked, playing innocent.

"Let's just cut to the chase," said Bunny. "Do you find Hunter attractive, and would you like to go on a date with him?"

She plunked her cup down on the saucer. "Wha' are you lot up to?" Last thing she'd expected was to be grilled at the tea party.

"We've seen the way you watch him when you think no one is looking. He's been teasing you mercilessly, and while you give it right back to him, you never seem to get really angry."

"I don't watch him," she huffed.

"Yes, you do, dear. And he watches you," Bunny said, and bit into a tea sandwich.

"He does not." She blew out a breath. "Does he?" she asked.

All three women nodded. "He does."

"No. I don't believe it. Besides, he's been seeing Carley."

Kelsey shook her head. "No, he's been *flirting* with her, and I don't believe he intends to ask her out."

"But if Carley wants him, she'll get him. I've not worked with her before, but I've heard she *always* gets what she wants." She winced, realizing she sounded petulant.

"It takes two to tango, and I don't think he wants her to *get him*, as you say. We all—" Frankie gestured to the three of them "—think he's interested in you."

"But I'm leaving before too long. As soon as I do the last few stunts, I'll be on my way and looking for the next job."

"Ha! That's what you think. We each came here for a short stay," Kelsey said. "I was planning a couple of months at most to be Nash's physical therapist last summer. Yet look at me now." She waved the hand with her wedding ring, then pointed to her pregnant belly.

"I came along with Kelsey, knowing we'd be moving on. But Angus and I fell in love and got married. So here I am to stay," Bunny said.

Mackenzie looked at Frankie, waiting for her story.

"I was supposed to be here for two weeks to work on a merger. Fell for Wyatt—literally, right smack in the mud—and here we are now, a family," Frankie said.

"But…"

"Our point is, if you and Hunter are meant to be together, it'll happen," Kelsey said.

"We're not meant to be together." Mackenzie sighed. "Oh, all right. Yes, I find him attractive. Yes, I like him. A lot. But Carley is beautiful and glamorous and famous. I'm a tomboy, and more often than not I'm covered in dirt and mud, smell like a horse and can't tame this unruly mess of hair." She grabbed a fistful of hair and shook it.

The women all smiled, and it kind of scared her.

"We can help you with that," Bunny said, and sipped her tea.

"Why?" Mackenzie asked.

"Why what?" Frankie set her cup and saucer down on the table.

"Why would you want to help me *get* Hunter? It's not as if you know me."

"Just call it women's intuition, but we think you're perfect for him," Kelsey said. "Besides, we like you. You'd fit in great with us."

"What if he doesn't want me? He seems to be doing fine being single."

"He needs to settle down. You—" Bunny pointed at her "—would be perfect for him."

"So what do I need to do?"

"Just sit back and relax. Let us do the work," Frankie said. "Operation Scotland commences now."

She agreed to let them help her, then wondered why. It wouldn't work.

Would it? A little glimmer of hope took root, and she almost hoped they were right.

Hunter leaned against the bar and tipped the beer bottle up. Ice-cold beer splashed over his tongue. It might be thirty degrees outside the barn—mild for this time of year—but cold beer was good any day.

Music played, tiny white lights twinkled overhead like stars in the rafters and people milled around the barn having a good time. So why wasn't he? Instead he was here, talking to his brothers, and wishing he was at home watching TV with his boys. And a certain Scottish lass.

At least he was off the hook with Carley. He knew now he'd never really been interested in her—if he had been, it would have hurt a little when she said she was going back with that Bryant guy.

He looked around the barn, searching for wild red hair.

"Who are you looking for?" Wyatt asked.

Hunter shrugged. "No one."

"Riiight," Nash drawled.

Hunter swung his head around to look at his oldest brother. "What's that supposed to mean?"

Nash shrugged. "Nothin'."

The door across from the bar opened, and Hunter stood on his toes, hoping…then saw Frankie slip inside, Bunny and Kelsey following close behind.

"Finally," Wyatt muttered.

"What's going on?" Hunter asked.

Kade grimaced. "Don't ask." He picked up his beer and walked toward the food table.

Kelsey joined them. "Mom and your dad want to keep the kids tonight since the party will probably run late. Hunter, you okay if the boys stay?"

"Sure. The kids all love the big sleepovers at Grandma and Gramp's house." Okay, so now he'd get to go home and watch TV. All alone.

The door opened again, and Hunter tried to look through the crowd, thought he caught a glimpse of red hair. Just as he started to walk that way, someone grabbed his arm.

"Hunter! Look!" Carley squealed.

He tried to shake her off, feeling as if he needed to be at the door.

"Hunter, pay attention to me."

He finally looked at Carley. She held her left hand toward him as if she wanted him to kiss it. "What?"

She lifted her hand up and pointed at her ring finger. Specifically at the giant diamond on her finger. "Bryant and I are engaged!"

"Hey, that's great," he said, and gave her a quick hug. "Best wishes."

"Thank you. I need to get back to my honey," Carley said, and hurried away from him.

He turned around to pick up his beer off the bar, and his gaze passed over a woman staring at him from the other end.

Whoa.

He looked again at the woman and realized it was Mackenzie. Only no Mackenzie he'd seen before. Her wild red hair had been pulled up into some fancy hairdo that left her graceful neck bare. She wore a dark green dress that hugged curves—curves that had previously been hidden behind jeans and bulky sweatshirts.

Plunking his beer back down, he started walking to her as she turned away from him. Giving him a view of a pair of killer legs. The dress ended at her knees, and her calves were set to stun by a pair of high-heeled shoes.

He quickened his pace and snagged her hand. "Hey, where you been?"

She yanked her hand back and turned around. The hurt on her face surprised him.

"I told them it was her you wanted."

"What? Who?" he asked, totally confused.

"Carley," she said.

"I don't want Carley."

"You were hugging her."

"Oh, that. She just told me she and Bryant are engaged. I was congratulating her."

She tugged at the low neckline of her dress, trying to pull it up. "I told them this wouldn't work—" She stilled, dropped her arms. "Carley's engaged? To Bryant?"

He nodded. The more he looked at her, the more he wished there weren't a million people filling the barn. He wanted to be alone with her. In the hayloft. In his truck. Hell, anywhere but here.

"You look beautiful," he said, low enough she had to lean forward to hear him. And she did look beautiful. She'd done something with her makeup so her eyes looked sexy and mysterious. Red defined the lips he'd been thinking about constantly for days on end. Her normally untamed curls were gathered up off her neck, and she looked very feminine.

"I don't. It's just outer trappings—"

"You're beautiful."

Her cheeks colored, and she looked down. "Well, thanks for that."

"Dance?"

"What?"

"Dance with me," he said as he held his hand out.

She stared at his hand for so long he started to think she wouldn't take it. Slowly she reached out to him, and he folded her fingers into his. He pulled her to the dance floor just as the music went from some fast country song to a slow ballad.

Perfect.

He swung her into his arms, held her close. She fit

just right against his body. He moved in time to the music, and she followed him.

They were such different people—he was a cowboy, for shootin' sake, and she was a brave Scottish redhead. How was it they fit together as good as apple pie and ice cream?

He focused on her, the way she felt as she moved. The music played as if just for them. They could have been the only two people in the barn.

She angled her head to rest her chin on his shoulder. Her hair brushed his cheek as she nestled a little closer to him. It smelled of sunshine, and was soft as satin. He wanted to pull the pins out one by one, and let her curls down so his hands could dive into her hair and just feel.

Sliding his hand down her back, he rested his fingers at the base of her spine, nudged her just a bit closer to him.

He knew in that moment he wanted her. Had to have her.

And hoped to God she wanted him back.

Chapter 13

After the party, Hunter pulled into the driveway of his cabin. He hopped out, hurried around to open Mackenzie's door and helped her out. They walked up the path to the front door, and he opened it, held it for her to pass by him.

She stopped in the foyer, and he slid her big puffy coat off. Then he could see her again in that dress that showed off her body.

Even as he turned around, he caught her tugging the neckline up for the twentieth time that night. "That's not your dress, is it?"

She dropped her hand. "Why do you ask?"

"Because you haven't seemed to be comfortable all evening."

"You're right. Frankie loaned it to me for the dance."

He nodded as if he understood, but knew better than to ask why. It hadn't been a formal party—everyone else had worn jeans tonight, including him. Hell, he'd barely had time to change into a clean T-shirt and flannel.

Walking ahead of her, he turned the lights on in the

living room, but dimmed the switch a bit so they weren't on full brightness.

Her shoes clicked on the floor behind him, her footsteps sounding tentative.

"Are you tired?" he asked, hoping she'd say no. He didn't want to leave her yet.

"Not really. Are you?"

"Nope."

"Oh."

Jeez, they'd be standing in the living room doorway all night at this rate. "Wanna play a game?"

She bit her lip. "What kind of game?"

For some reason he thought she was thinking he'd say something naughty and was scared to death. "Gin rummy, dominoes, a trivia game, video game?" He grinned. "Candyland?"

She looked surprised, then laughed. "Your boys have Candyland?"

"I bought it for them for Christmas. Since Maddy always wins, I figured they could practice at home."

"Brilliant."

"Why don't you go change, get comfortable? Popcorn? Hot chocolate?"

"Sounds good. Be right back."

He watched her walk away, wondering if she realized the high heels made her butt sway back and forth just a little. He watched, fascinated, and turned as she disappeared down the hallway.

He went into the kitchen and fixed their snacks. She'd dressed up for him—at least he hoped it was for him. She hadn't looked at anyone else at the party tonight, hadn't left his side since she arrived.

Not that he'd have let her go anyway.

By the time the scent of buttered popcorn filled the

kitchen, she was back, wearing yoga pants and a sweatshirt, face freshly scrubbed, her glorious hair down around her shoulders.

"Smells good in here," she said.

"Good timing," he said, picked up the tray and led the way to the couch by the fireplace.

He set the tray on the coffee table, then lit a match to the waiting logs. Settling back on the couch, he felt like he had on his first date. Only now he was an adult, the girl he liked was a grown woman and no one's dad lurked in the other room.

He glanced at Mackenzie. She was sitting up straight at the other end of the couch, looking as uncomfortable as he felt.

"This is ridiculous," he muttered.

Just as she turned to him, he reached over and picked up her slippered feet. He put them on the coffee table, grabbed the bowl of popcorn and sat closer to her, putting his own feet up.

"Relax," he said, and shoved a handful of popcorn in his mouth. He held the bowl between them, and gradually felt her relax next to him.

"I'm sorry," she finally said.

"For what?"

"I don't do this much."

"Eat popcorn in front of a crackling fire?"

She chucked a kernel of popcorn at him, and it hit his nose.

"No. Eat popcorn in front of the fire with an attractive man," she said, then took a drink of hot chocolate.

"You think I'm attractive?"

She rolled her eyes, and he liked that she was finally comfortable enough to do that.

"No, actually I don't," she said.

"You *don't* find me attractive?" he asked, surprised at the shot of hurt he felt, and purposely pouted.

She turned sideways and tucked her feet up on the couch. "Nope. I think you're wildly hot, incredibly funny, kind and so sweet it makes my teeth hurt."

He set the bowl on the table, let her words sink in. "I'm wildly hot?"

She sputtered a laugh. "Is that all you heard?"

He waved a hand. "I heard the other stuff. It's the hot part that makes me want to do this." He took her in his arms and lay them both down.

He kissed her once, twice, then paused, watching her face. Her expression went from surprised to sensual in five seconds flat.

"Then by all means, proceed," she said, and pulled his head down.

He dove right in and kissed her, encouraged when she met his lips with a hunger of her own. Her tongue darted out and touched his, shyly, then slid away.

He cradled her head gently, angled his own to take it deeper. She was like no one he'd ever been with before. Fun, exciting, she didn't take his shit, and spoke up when she felt something was wrong.

Finally indulging himself, he threaded his fingers through her hair. It was soft and silky, exactly how he'd known it would be.

His body was so hot, so hard, he thought he'd explode. But he didn't want to scare her away. Yeah, she'd admitted she found him hot. Didn't mean she was ready for more.

Was he?

He eased back, his breath heaving as much as hers was. He took his time, kissing her nose, her eyelids, her cheeks. His thumb stroked her neck, and her pulse jumped beneath it.

"Mackenzie," he groaned.

It took a few seconds until she finally opened her eyes, looked at him. "Yes?"

"I want you," he said, but before he could go on, he felt her body tense beneath him. Which gave him his answer. "But I don't want us to do anything until you're completely comfortable with me. With us."

"Is there an *us*?" she asked so softly he had to strain to hear it.

"I'd like to explore that. If you want to."

She smiled, then the light in her eyes dimmed. "But I'll be leaving before long."

"Then maybe we should explore a relationship faster."

"Faster?"

"Yeah, like light speed faster. I don't know how long I can keep away from you."

Her smile came back, and grew and grew until she was laughing so hard he felt it through his own body.

He pulled back. "What's so dang funny?"

"I just got the vision of us moving in fast motion—eating and drinking at supersonic speed, dancing, taking long but very fast walks. Like if you fast-forward through a show on the telly."

He laughed. "Yeah, see? Great minds think alike. The only thing I don't want to speed up is kissing you. Deal?"

"Oh, aye. I agree with that one, boyo." She grinned and lifted her head up enough to kiss him.

Damn.

What an amazing woman. Did he have the right to ask her for this?

Did he really want to explore a relationship with her when Montana wasn't her home?

He looked down at her, smiling.

God help him, he did.

***

Mackenzie tossed and turned for what seemed like hours in her bed. Alone. She knew it was good that she and Hunter hadn't gone any further, but she was still frustrated. Aching for him, she finally relaxed enough to drift off to sleep.

Smoke filled her lungs till she was near bursting. Her eyes streamed, and she couldn't see anything—none of the safety equipment to make sure she could escape unharmed. Her voice was so weak she couldn't cry for help.

She pounded on the door, desperate for someone to hear her. Kicking her legs didn't help; something had trapped her on the ground.

She didn't want to die, leave her brothers all alone. She had to be there for them. See them grow up, get married, have children. Putting as much energy as she could into it, she tried screaming again.

Someone was shaking her, shouting her name. That hadn't happened before.

"Mackenzie! Wake up. Come on, honey, wake up."

She opened her eyes, filled her lungs with fresh air, then coughed. Remnants of the dream clung tight, and she tried to shake her head, get it free of the terror.

"You okay? You back now?" Hunter asked, holding her in his arms.

"Where are we?"

"Your room. I heard you screaming. It was a dream." He rocked her back and forth. "You're okay now. Shh, shh, shh," he whispered, until she could finally release some of the tension holding her so rigid.

"It wasn't just a dream. It really happened." She pulled away from him, shoved the twisted blanket and sheets off her legs. That must have been why she felt trapped.

"What do you mean?"

"Stunt gone wrong. Months ago." She coughed again.

Hunter got up and went to the bathroom, brought a glass filled with water to her.

She sipped, thankful for the icy cold water as it soothed her raw throat. Then she said, "I'm sorry I woke you."

He walked around to the other side of the bed, climbed in and pulled her into his arms. "Want to talk about it?" he asked, and she rested her head against his shoulder.

She hesitated, then remembered what a therapist had said. *Get it out in the open, take the power away from the terror.* "We were rehearsing one of the stunts. The lead actress was supposed to be trapped in a closet in a burning building. The fire that was supposed to be contained suddenly wasn't, and I got trapped. The door jammed and I couldn't get out. The stunt coordinator finally realized something was wrong, and they had to break the door down."

"Shit," he muttered, his arms tightening around her. "How long?"

"Felt like hours, but it was only a few minutes, from what they said. They had extinguishers and put the fire out. But I was burned so I had to spend time in hospital."

"God, I'm so sorry, honey."

"It's okay now. I'm okay now." She nestled her head on his sturdy shoulder, wished she'd had it—him—when she was going through all that.

"Is that what those marks on the backs of your thighs are from?" he asked.

"How did you—oh, right." Embarrassment flooded her all over again that he'd seen her naked.

"I'm sorry. I shouldn't have asked."

"They're kind of hard to miss."

"Are those the only scars?"

"Some smaller ones on my stomach, but the legs were the worst. Closer to the fire."

"I've been meaning to ask how you got to be a stunt-woman."

"A movie was being filmed in Aberdeen, and one day a production assistant happened to be passing by when I was teaching a tumbling class and asked me to audition. I got the job, thinking it was just for that movie. The director passed my name along to someone else who was looking for a woman who could ride, so I got that job. After several other recommendations, one of the stunt coordinators suggested I go to Hollywood where I could find steadier work, so here I am."

"What do your brothers think about it?"

"They tease me about being on screen and no one knows it's me, but I think they're proud of me. I don't always tell them about some of the stunts—even though they're younger than me, they're pretty protective."

"Have you ever thought of getting into another line of work?"

She sat up and looked at him. "I know how to do my job," she snapped.

"Hey, I know you do. You're very much a professional, and you've worked hard to get where you are. I care about you. I just don't want you to get hurt."

She studied him. He was all rumpled, hair sticking straight up on one side. His T-shirt was wrinkled, he wore dark blue pajama bottoms with polar bears dancing on them, and his feet were bare.

And she wanted him.

Bad.

She just had to make sure her heart was protected this time.

Chapter 14

Hunter opened the door to his cabin, and walked in to loud voices and something that smelled so good his mouth watered.

He dropped his packages and followed his nose to the kitchen, not sure what to expect. Certainly not Mackenzie at the stove, her hair pulled up in a messy knot, steam rising from a pot as she stirred, his boys sitting at the counter, all trying to talk over each other. She was laughing at something they were saying, and as she turned around, he was struck again by how pretty she was.

Soft curls had escaped the knot and framed her face, no makeup, smiling brighter than the sun, and the way she looked at his sons was…

Awesome. It was the only word that penetrated the fog in his brain.

When she noticed him, her smile grew even bigger. "Good evenin'."

"What's going on?" he asked.

"I thought I'd make dinner tonight. I hope that's fine wi' ye."

"Sure. What are you making?" he asked, a little worried since she'd said her brothers loved haggis.

"Beef stew and bannocks," she said, and opened the oven door.

"Bannocks? Is that like haaaagis?" Tripp asked, making the word so guttural Hunter was surprised he didn't spit everywhere.

She turned from the oven, holding a pan. "No, silly, it's what you Americans call biscuits." She held the pan up for them to see, then dumped them in a basket lined with a cloth napkin.

Turning around, he saw the table was set all festive-like.

Was it a holiday? Someone's birthday?

Shit.

Maybe he could sneak out and get a gift—

Where? It was after six o'clock, snowing, and she'd already seen him.

"You want to wash up for dinner?" Mackenzie asked him.

"Oh, sure. Be right back." He headed to his bedroom and yanked off his cold-weather gear, then pulled his boots off. While he washed his hands, he tried to think what he could do for her, since she'd gone to so much work already.

Man, he hadn't had a woman, other than Mrs. Green, cook for him since his divorce. He could get used to this…

Walking back out to the living room, he saw the grocery bags he'd dumped on the table. Picking one up, he saw sprigs of something poking out. Mrs. Green periodically sent vegetables home with him, convinced all he fed his sons were toaster pastries, hot dogs and potato chips.

He grabbed the other bag and went back to his bedroom, dumped everything out on his bed and sorted through it. Herbs and vegetables. *A little bunch of this, a little bunch of that, some purply stalky thing and some of the other stuff.* He shoved them all into a bouquet of sorts, and searched for something to hold it all together. He finally settled on a narrow leather strip, tying it best he could into a bow.

He shoved everything back into the bags and carried them to the kitchen, set them on the counter.

"You're just in time. Have a seat," Mackenzie said.

The boys all popped off the bar stools and sat on the bench. No shoving, no pushing, no arguing.

He leaned closer to her. "Who are these boys, and where are my kids?"

She grinned. "They've been very sweet today."

He brought his arm around from behind his back and held the bouquet out to her. "I wanted to get you fresh flowers, but we're a little short on them this time of year."

Her mouth opened and formed a perfect O, and she took the bouquet from him, then buried her face in it. She inhaled, and finally looked up at him, beaming. "Thank you."

"You like it?"

She sniffed it again. "It reminds me of my granny's kitchen from so long ago." She stood on tiptoe and kissed his cheek. "You're a verra sweet man."

He'd have to remember to thank Mrs. Green.

Mackenzie brought the stew pot to the table and filled everyone's bowls, then brought the biscuits and sat down. She set the bouquet next to her plate on the table.

"What's that?" Tripp asked.

"Your da brought herbs for me."

The boys looked at him like he was nuts. "Why'd you do that?" Cody asked.

"I thought she might like them," he said.

She picked up the bouquet and held it toward the boys. "Just smell the wonderful scents from these fresh herbs. Parsley, sage, rosemary and thyme." She pointed at each one. "I can use them next time I make dinner. And whatever's left, I can press in a book and take it home with me to remember my time here."

The boys looked at each other, then got up and ran around the table to where she sat. "We don't want you to leave. You have to stay," they said, voices crowding each other.

"Hey, guys," he said, hating how sad they looked. "Miss Mackenzie doesn't live here. She has to go back home so she can be in other movies. You wouldn't want her to miss out on more adventures, would you?"

"N-n-n-o-o-o." Eli sniffled. "But we love her."

"Oh, boys. I love you, too," Mackenzie said, and gathered them close in a hug. "I'll write to you, and send postcards, and email, if that's okay." She looked up at him, and he nodded.

Damn, he didn't want her to leave either.

"Okay, boys. Sit down and eat." He waited till they'd settled back down, this time with the pushing and the shoving, then picked up his spoon and tried the stew. Rich and savory, it was different from anything he'd had before. "Hey, this is really good."

"Don't sound so surprised. Did you think I'd make something disgusting?" she asked, grinning at him. "If I did, then I'd have to eat it, too. And I don't know about you, but I don't like gross stuff." She made a face and the boys laughed.

They ate in silence, which meant the boys actually

liked the stew. He'd have to get the recipe from her before she left. Which sent a little pang through his gut.

They needed a distraction.

"Boys, how about we set out early tomorrow and ride the fence line?"

The boys cheered.

"What does that mean?" Mackenzie asked.

"We have to ride along the fence constantly, make sure nothing is broken so our herd doesn't wander off. My brothers and I split up the acreage and ride out weekly. The boys are learning what it takes to be ranchers. They'll inherit all of this one day, with their cousins, and I'm teaching them what they need to know."

She was quiet for a moment. "Think my horse and I could ride out with you? We'd both like to see more of your land, get some fresh air."

He wondered at the wistful look on her face. She seemed almost sad.

Sliding his hand across the table, he squeezed her fingers lightly. "You okay?"

She gave him a watery smile. "Yes. Just missing Scotland. Some parts of your ranch remind me of home."

"Are you working tomorrow?"

She shook her head. "We went o'er the schedule earlier, and the director is filming inside scenes tomorrow, so I'm no' needed."

He grinned. "Okay, it's a date. The more the merrier. But we'll be setting out early."

She beamed. "Brilliant. I'll be ready."

Wow. If he'd known it was that easy to make her smile like that, he'd have asked her to ride the fence ages ago. Because in the last couple of days, it had suddenly become important to him to make her smile.

* * *

The next morning Mackenzie took up the rear of the little group as they left the barn on horseback. She breathed deeply, inhaling air so cold it made her lungs hurt. It was what she'd grown up on, so this part really did remind her of the Highlands. The forecast said it would warm up today, but she much preferred the cold.

Clouds hung low, melding with snow-covered hills on the horizon. Occasional breaks in the clouds showed her the mountains rising high, standing silent and tall.

Ahead of her, the boys rode single file behind their dad, who broke the snow on the trail for them. The kids wore their usual colors, but she'd gotten to know them enough now she could tell them apart even without the distinguishing colors.

They plowed through the snow, farther and farther from the ranch buildings. She hadn't realized how big the Sullivan ranch was. The snow blanketed all sound, but she bet it was quiet like that even in summer.

Ahead of her, Hunter raised his hand, and the boys all reined in their horses. She dismounted when he did, and her feet slid down a small embankment into a four-foot-high drift. She tried stepping out of it, but it didn't help. Tried to walk forward, but the snow was too packed by then.

Stuck.

She swiveled all around, looking for something to give her traction, then caught Hunter watching her, grinning.

"Well, don't just stand there laughing like a loon. Help me out," she huffed.

"It'd be my pleasure," he said, and forged a path to her. He put his hands on her waist and as he lifted her, she reached up and put her arms around his neck. Free of the snow, she wrapped her legs around his waist as he carried her away.

Even as bundled up as they were, she felt a little wicked being held this way, and almost wished they were alone. And naked.

"You keep moving on me like that, and I'll have to lay facedown in the snow," he whispered in her ear.

She stopped moving, held herself rigid. "Maybe I can help with that." She pulled his collar back, shoved the fistful of snow she'd grabbed down his back.

"Hey!" he shouted.

"You said you needed to cool off." She smirked.

He shifted, and suddenly she went sailing through the air, landing flat on her back in another snowdrift.

She laughed up at the gray sky. Hunter's face appeared above her.

"Now who's laughing like a loon. You all right, Mackenzie?" he asked.

"Aye, dandy."

"You wanna get up outta the snow?"

"Sure."

He extended a gloved hand and pulled her up.

Little-boy giggles broke the silence, and she looked behind her. The Triples were pelting each other with snowballs.

"Hey, boys. Saddle up. Work first, play later."

She mounted Rory again and settled into the easy rhythm of his gait. Hunter had told her earlier that morning that teaching the boys about the ranch would count toward school credit, even as young as they were. She wished her schooling had been like that, instead of stuck inside a classroom all day.

Hunter pulled up again at a line of fence that had

fallen down. They all dismounted, and she watched as he taught the boys what had to be done. It wasn't so much wanting to know how to fix a fence in the middle of a ranch. It was more wanting to watch this man be so patient with his boys.

He'd gently correct one if he did it wrong, and never lost his temper. He was also quick to praise their work. Sometimes she thought he was just a big kid himself, then he'd go and do something grown up, be responsible, be a good father.

She turned away.

"Hey, you okay?" he asked, coming into her watery line of sight.

"Sure, just got something in my eye." She pulled a glove off, then rubbed a hand over her eyes again.

"Did something upset you? Your eyes are red."

Biting her lip to quell the sob didn't help, and she flung herself into his arms. He caught her before they fell backward, and rubbed a hand up and down her back.

"It's okay. Whatever it is. I'll fix it," he murmured.

"There's nothing to fix." She leaned back, looked him in the face. "You're a great da. These boys are verra lucky to have you." Pulling out of his embrace, she hurried to her horse and got on.

Chancing a peek at him, she saw he still stood in the same spot, a dumbfounded look on his face.

"Come on then, boyo. There are fences to be mended," she called.

He mounted Becket, and they set off.

The morning wore on, and they'd stopped at least fifteen times to mend fences before Hunter called for a break.

She slid off her horse and stomped her feet, rubbed her hands together.

Hunter pulled two thermoses out of his saddlebag. He poured out of one and handed it to her, and the rich fragrant scent of the coffee he liked drifted to her nose.

And isn't it scary that I know what type of coffee he favors? She sipped and blinked at how strong it was, and shuddered as it went down. She usually preferred tea. "That'll put hair on your chest," she muttered.

"If it does, you can borrow my razor," Hunter said behind her.

She jumped, and coffee sloshed over onto her glove.

He snickered. "Coffee too strong?"

"How can you drink this and not go through the roof?"

"Oh, come on. Don't be a wimp."

She narrowed her eyes at him. "Who're you calling a wimp, boyo?"

He opened his mouth, but the tiniest mewling sound came from behind her. She held her hand up to silence him. "Did you hear that?"

"Hear what?"

She strained her ears trying to hear it again. Then it sounded again, only it came from above her. She looked up into towering trees. Finally, she spotted movement in one tree.

She pointed up. "There's a cat way up there. How the bloody heck did it manage to get all the way up there?"

"It's a cat. They climb."

She flicked him a disgusted look. "I know that, bampot. But there aren't any low-hanging branches." She moved toward the tree. "Come here, kitty," she called to it.

The cat just stared down at her, shivering.

"We need to get her down. She's freezing."

Hunter looked from her to the tree, and back to her. "How do you propose I do that?"

She grabbed the rope from Hunter's saddle and slung it over her shoulder, then whistled for Rory. He trotted to her side, and she positioned him at the tree. She tucked her parka into her jeans as best she could, then swung up into the saddle. Pulling her legs in, she stood up on Rory's back.

"What are you doing?" Hunter hissed at her. "Get down from there."

"Just hold him steady." She balanced, looking up to the lowest branch. Sliding the rope off her shoulder, she let out several lengths, then tossed it up, praying it would go right the first time.

The rope sailed upward, then went over the branch, sending a shower of snow onto her face. She brushed it off, then reached for the other side of the rope.

She looked down at Hunter. "Here I go."

"Be careful."

She winked at him. Grateful she had on her thick gloves, she started walking up the tree trunk, pulling herself up with the rope. When she reached the first set of branches, she stepped off onto one, and pulled herself up into the next section.

Leaning forward, she tested another branch. It snapped off in her hand, and she almost slipped. She grabbed another handhold and steadied herself.

Almost there. Keep going. Don't look down. She looked down. Hunter and the Triples stared up at her. From very far away.

She shut her eyes, blew out a breath and centered herself.

A plaintive meow sounded closer now, and she opened her eyes to see the tabby cat eyeing her. "Come ón, sweetie. I'm here to take you home, okay?" She made kissy-kissy noises and wiggled her fingers. The cat crept forward and sniffed the tips of her gloved fingers, then backed away.

"Now don't be stubborn, baby. Come to me." She wiggled her fingers again, and the cat stretched its head out to sniff again. It crept forward a little more, enough so she could grab it by the scruff, which elicited a very undignified hiss.

"Oh, shut up. You must be a boy kitty. Can't ever be rescued by a woman, huh?" She pulled it into a hug, holding it till it stopped hissing and snuggled into her warmth.

"There we go. That's no' so bad now, eh?" She unzipped her parka enough to guide the cat inside, then zipped it back up. The cat shifted, then snuggled right in.

Retracing her movements down the branches, section by section, she finally reached her rope. She gripped it and began a slow rappel back down, making sure she didn't startle the cat.

At one point the cat shifted around, then poked its head out by her neck, sniffed and stuck it back inside.

She gauged how much farther she had to go, then was finally close enough to step on Rory's back. She let go of the rope and sat down, then dismounted.

The boys jumped up and down, cheering.

"Can we see it?" Eli asked.

She unzipped her parka enough for the boys to see the cat, who shrank back against her. "You know what? This poor kitty is probably hungry and thirsty. How about we go home and get it settled? Then I'll bet it will let you pet it."

She looked up at Hunter, who was coiling the rope, his back to her.

The boys ran to their horses and mounted up.

"Thanks for your help," she said to Hunter.

He briefly glanced at her. "You could have been killed."

She stepped back, her heart pounding so hard she thought it would burst. "I knew what I was doing—"

"This is real life. Not a movie set where you have safety precautions in place. There was nothing I could have done if you'd fallen except try to catch you."

She backed up another step, angry that he hadn't trusted her.

"Did you even stop to think how that would have affected my children if you'd fallen and died in front of them?"

Chapter 15

She whipped her head sideways to look at the kids. They were on their horses, leaning toward each other, whispering.

"Nothing happened."

"You're right. This time. You can't keep risking your life like this."

"Who are you to bloody tell me what I can and can't do?" Her voice cracked, and she cleared her throat, swallowed a sob. "This is *my* job. It's not your place to boss me around, to say I can't do it."

"Look, I'm sorry. I was worried, okay?"

She stomped around him and swung up into Rory's saddle. The cat squirmed against her, and she rested a hand on it, patting it till it settled down again. Nudging Rory, she guided him around to what she hoped was the way back to the ranch. The fence had been on her left the whole way, so she kept it on her right.

Before long she heard the crunch of the other horses behind her, and Hunter trotted in front to lead the way.

The boys were actually subdued. They could probably tell their dad was upset.

The long ride back to the ranch didn't do much to calm her down. She wondered what was going through Hunter's head.

The cat hadn't moved much, content with her body heat. By the time they reached the ranch, she was cold and hungry, and more than ready to be off a horse. But instead of turning the way she'd expected, Hunter led them to a big cabin and barn she hadn't seen before.

The front door opened, and Luke walked out. "Hey, what's going on?"

Hunter came up to her and held his hand out. "I figured we ought to bring the cat straight to Luke. Make sure it's okay."

She unzipped her coat enough to pull the cat out and handed it to Hunter.

It hissed at him, even as he crooned to it. Then he handed the cat to Luke. "Found this cat out while we were riding the fence."

Luke scratched the cat's chin, and it settled right against him. "Where was it?"

The boys all piped up, talking over each other to tell the story. Luke finally looked up with a *what the hell* expression on his face.

Hunter said something to Luke, who nodded. "Guys, you want to stay with me, help me check the cat out? We'll need to clean it up, take some pictures to send out, see if it belongs around here." Luke and the boys disappeared inside while Hunter led their horses inside the barn.

This was her chance to get some much-needed space. She wheeled Rory around and galloped back to the barn where his stall was. She sped through the routine of taking care of him, making sure he was okay but desperate not to see Hunter.

She caught a ride with one of the ranch hands, who dropped her at Hunter's cabin. Relieved to see he wasn't there yet, she hurried to her room and shut the door. Tired, dirty, cold and, she realized, scratched, all she wanted was a hot bath.

Shedding her outerwear, she sat and pulled her boots off. She stripped down to her panties and tank top, and went into the en suite bathroom. Turning on the tub faucet, she stuck her hand under the water, hoping it would heat quickly.

A door slammed in the cabin, and seconds later, someone pounded on her bedroom door.

It could only be Hunter.

She ignored the knock.

He banged on the door again.

She ignored it again.

This time he hammered on the door and wouldn't let up.

Bloody cowboy.

She shut the water faucets off and stomped out of the bathroom and to the bedroom door. "What do you want?" she hollered, flinging the door open.

"Don't ignore me," Hunter said. His eyes flashed anger and hurt, and it shocked her.

"Then don't patronize me. You're not my father or my boss. Ye canna tell me wha' to do."

"I'm not trying to tell you what to do. Don't you get it?" he shouted. He flung his hat down.

"Get what?" she asked, backing up.

He strode toward her and stopped in front of her so close she fought to breathe. "I don't want you to die!" He cupped her cheeks. "I care about you."

"No," she said, and tried to move back.

But he wouldn't let her go.

"Yes, dammit. I didn't want to. But I do." He kissed her, hard, and she tasted his anger on his lips.

She fought back, kissing him with her own Scottish anger.

He let go of her cheeks to pull her body flush to his. He was hot, hard, and she wanted to curl up and stay there forever.

But she couldn't. She was finally free of responsibilities. Her brothers were grown, or almost, and she could do what she wanted with her life. She liked working on movies, liked the change of pace, the action, the process of working out stunts.

His lips slid over hers, his tongue chased hers, and it drove her crazy. She suddenly wasn't cold any longer. Heat bloomed inside her and turned liquid, languid. She wanted to see him naked, feel that magnificent body skin to skin, muscle to muscle—man to woman.

He cupped her arse, lifting her against him. She shifted her hips, cradling his hardness with her body, and he groaned.

He walked her backward until the backs of her knees hit the bed. "God, I want you," he whispered, all traces of anger in his words gone.

His words sent a flood of emotions rioting through her head. Her body. Her heart.

Desire, yes.

Want, yes.

Need, saints be praised, *yes*.

And fear.

She wasn't afraid of *him*.

She was afraid of herself.

She'd kept her emotions tight to her chest all these years, afraid to trust anyone but her closest kin. Her mother's words about not trusting men, and her own experience with that actor, had made her skittish.

But with Hunter, she knew instinctively she could trust him. And the knowledge cooled her ire even as her desire flamed to life.

"I want you, too," she whispered.

He pulled back just enough to look at her, almost surprised, and she wondered why.

"Then that's a good thing, isn't it?" He lifted her up and tossed her onto the bed, then followed, covering her body with his.

His weight was welcome, warming her from the inside out. She felt wanton, wicked.

He lifted his head, looked down at her. "You're not wearing many clothes."

"And you're wearing too many."

"I can fix that," he said, and stood up.

"By all means, do." She propped her hands under her head and gazed at him.

He started unbuttoning his blue flannel shirt, then looked up at her. "What're you doing?"

"Watching the show."

His eyebrows popped up, then he grinned, looking decidedly naughty.

Oh, goody! Her girlie parts took notice as he started stripping his clothes off, putting on a show.

The long-sleeved shirt came off. Then he started sliding the black thermal shirt up his stomach, revealing those hard abs she'd only felt before. His chest muscles made her want to sing, but she restrained herself and licked her lips.

He yanked the shirt off, then whirled it around his head and let it fly to the other side of the bed.

"Wow," she murmured, eyeing his chest and abs.

"You like?" he asked, and struck a muscle pose.

She laughed. "Oh, go on wi' ye."

Hard work over the years had honed his body into a Greek-god-worthy physique. She rolled her eyes at herself for going all poetic. If he knew what she was thinking, his already inflated ego would burst.

He put his hands on his belt buckle and looked at her.

She lifted her hand and waved her fingers. "Proceed."

He grinned, slid the strap out of the loop, then flipped the strap back with flair to pull it from the prong. Sliding the rest of the strap from the buckle, he whipped it out of all the belt loops, threw it over his shoulder.

Twisting first one way, then the other, he struck a couple of bodybuilder poses.

She scrambled up from her reclining position to lie on her stomach, facing him. She propped her chin in her hands, and batted her eyelashes at him.

He slid his hands down his stomach to the button on his jeans, and she went still. Then he shook a finger at her and turned around to face the other way.

"Hey," she protested. "Wha' are ye doin'?"

He moved his bottom back and forth, and peered over his shoulder at her.

She'd never imagined foreplay could be this much fun, and they'd hardly touched each other. Excitement built, and she couldn't wait to see what he did next.

A zipper sound rasped in the air, and he shimmied his backside some more. He slowly slid his jeans down over his hips, then paused.

"Why'd you stop?" she asked, making her words very saucy.

He half turned, put a finger in the air. "Be right back," he said, and plopped on the floor.

What on earth?

One boot went flying over the bed to land on the other side. Then the next was tossed backward toward the windows.

He popped back up to his feet and assumed what she thought he thought she would think was a sexy pose. She grinned and went back to enjoying the show.

Sliding his jeans down farther revealed bright white briefs, then muscled legs, until he finally stepped out of them. Hands on hips, he looked at her, his mouth quirked. He shoved the covers back and got into bed then slid her toward him. He grabbed the blankets up to cover them both. "It's frickin' cold in here. Why didn't you build a fire?"

"Because someone had me boiling mad. And then verra turned on."

He grinned. "I turned you on?"

"Yes, you bam—"

He laid a finger on her lips. "Hey, no name-calling in the bedroom."

"What if I want to call you stud muffin?"

He tilted his head, looked up. "I suppose that would do."

"How about hot cowboy?"

He pursed his lips. "That would work."

She laughed. "Ye're a goofy man, Hunter Sullivan. I like you very much."

"That's a good thing, because I like you very much, Mackenzie Campbell." He kissed her then, and she forgot about playing games.

Cocooned beneath the blankets, she got lost in him. He'd antagonized her, bossed her around, teased her, charmed her and now seduced her. He was a complex man, and she'd grown to care about him in such a short time.

She'd told him she liked him, but if she admitted it to

herself, deep inside her heart, she more than liked him. She already loved his sons.

But what did she know about love? Her parents had never really seemed to be in love.

He rolled her over onto her back and kissed her until she was near dizzy with want.

"You're beautiful," he said.

"I dinna ken what to say when you tell me that," she said.

"Why? You are beautiful."

She shook her head. "No, I'm not. I'm a plain country girl. Not pretty like Carley."

"Stop," he said. "You are beautiful. You have more depth than any ten Carleys. You're brave, bold, beautiful and don't take my shit."

"I'm no' very experienced with men," she whispered. Heat bloomed in her cheeks, and she just knew she looked bright red.

"So the men you've been around are morons and didn't see the real you."

She bit her lip and looked away. "Well…"

"How many men have there been?"

"That's kind of rude to ask, isn't it?" She shut her eyes. "Just one."

"Yeah?"

"A few years ago, not long after I moved to America. Wooed me on a dare, but I didn't realize until it was too late." She shook her head, wanted to crawl into a hole. She'd never been so embarrassed before.

"Why now?" he asked, his voice husky.

She opened her eyes and met his gaze. "Wha'?"

"You've waited, not wanting to be with another man all these years. We don't have to do anything. We can just lie here—and cuddle," he said.

"No, I don't think so. Not when you've got me right where you want me. And I, you." She smiled.

"Then why? Why do you want this, between us?"

"Because I've never trusted any man like I trust you."

Chapter 16

Hours later, and Mackenzie's words about trusting him still rang in Hunter's head. They'd spent hours in her bed, and it had been amazing. Powerful.

He opened the refrigerator door, looked inside for something to cook for dinner, but wasn't seeing food. Images of Mackenzie laughing, then lost in passion, flooded his head.

He'd dated a few women since his divorce, but even though he had a reputation that said otherwise, he'd been very discreet and choosy about actually taking a relationship this far. And he'd felt nothing close to what he felt for Mackenzie with anyone else.

And just what was that? Was it enough to sustain a long-distance relationship?

He had to be sure, because it wasn't just him now. He had three kids who came first, and he wasn't about to start a relationship that would end up hurting them.

He shut the fridge door, opened the freezer, hoping he still had a frozen casserole or something from Mrs. Green.

Of course the sticking point was whether Mackenzie even wanted a relationship with him. Her home base was in LA, and she traveled all over working as a stuntwoman. Would she want to settle down on a ranch in Montana?

It scared him that she had such a dangerous job. Her antics that day rescuing the cat had worried him. He had faith she knew how to do her job, but that was after rehearsing with a coordinator, making sure there were safeguards in place. Anything could have happened earlier—a weak tree limb, the cat attacking her and making her slip. She could have broken her neck. Sure she was cautious, but things could go wrong. She'd admitted it had when she was caught in a fire and gotten burned.

Thumps above his head startled Hunter, and he grabbed the frozen hamburger patties he'd been staring at for the last few minutes. Simple, easy, fast.

Luke had dropped the boys off earlier, and they couldn't stop talking about the cat. It was fine, and a neighbor was grateful their kitty had been found safe.

Hunter set the patties to thawing and headed upstairs to check on the boys. They'd spread all their pillows around the floor and tied their sheets together, hanging them from the safety rail on Tripp's bunk bed.

"What are you boys doing?"

"Playing stuntman!" Cody shouted from the top of the bunk.

"Cut it out, guys. Come on down and clean this up. Dinner's ready soon."

Great, now he had to worry about his boys emulating Mackenzie and getting hurt.

Mackenzie was in the kitchen slicing the buns he'd left on the counter. She'd showered, and her hair was still damp. She was fresh-faced and beaming.

"What're the boys up to?" she asked.

"Playing stuntman."

The hand holding the knife paused, and she looked up at him. "What did they do?"

"Tied sheets to the bunk railing and were going to climb up. Like you did today with the tree." He tried to keep his tone neutral, but even he heard the note of worry and accusation.

Her face paled, and she set the knife down very carefully. "I'm sorry."

"I know why you did it. You have a soft heart and couldn't stand to let the cat be lost. But my kids are impressionable And they adore you. They see you doing heroic things, and doing them perfectly, and they want to copy you, be like you."

She backed up till she hit the fridge. "I'll talk to them—"

"No. I'll do it. They're *my* kids."

Edging sideways till she made it around the island, she looked at her watch. "I have to go."

"Where?"

She hesitated. "Tom called for a meeting."

He glanced at the clock on the wall. "Now? It's eight o'clock."

"Last-minute changes for tomorrow."

"I'll run you up to the lodge."

She flung a hand up. "No."

"You can't walk up there alone. At night."

"He's sending someone to pick me up. I'm going to wait outside."

She wouldn't meet his eyes, and he had a strange feeling she was lying. "I can run you up there."

She shook her head, her curls bouncing. "See you later."

"Don't you want a burger?"

"Not hungry. I can get something at the lodge. Good night." And she hurried toward her room.

He knew he'd hurt her feelings, but he couldn't help it. The words had just poured out, and he hadn't been able to block them.

They'd been so happy earlier in each other's arms.

And he'd gone and screwed it up.

Mackenzie made it to the lodge, frozen, hungry, tired, angry and incredibly sad. She hated lying, but she didn't think Hunter would have let her leave the cabin otherwise.

The dining room was still open, and she was one of the last people to have dinner. She'd been seated by the fireplace and was grateful for the heat. Dawdling over her meal, she wanted to stay away from the cabin as long as she could. If there'd been any rooms available in the lodge, she'd have begged for one.

"Mackenzie," a voice behind her said.

She looked around and saw Kelsey walking toward her. "Hello. What are you doing up here?"

"Nash is in a meeting and I came up to see my mother. Are you here alone?"

"Yes," Mackenzie said, and pushed the rest of her stew away.

Kelsey pulled the other chair out and plopped down. "Whew. I swear my mother must be right and we're having a boy. And he's going to be a linebacker for the NFL." She rubbed her belly and leaned back in the chair.

"You don't know what you're having?"

"No, we decided to be surprised." She took a roll out of the basket and split it in half. "So what's wrong?"

Mackenzie looked at her. "What?"

"You're up here, alone, picking at your food and looking like you lost your best friend."

"It's nothing."

"No, it's something. You can talk to me, you know." Kelsey patted Mackenzie's hand.

She hesitated, not wanting to burden Hunter's sister-in-law, then found herself spilling the story in a flood of words. Except for the way she and Hunter had spent the afternoon.

Kelsey listened, her eyes wide.

"And now Hunter hates me because his boys are trying to copy me."

"First, he doesn't hate you. I've seen the way he looks at you. That is definitely not hate. Second, he's scared to death about being a full-time father now."

Mackenzie nodded. "We talked about that."

Kelsey's eyebrows popped up her forehead. "You did? That's progress. You know, Hunter was my first friend when we came here last summer."

"He was?"

"Yup. Nash had been injured in Afghanistan, lost his unit and was angry, bitter and bit the head off everyone who came close. Including me. Hunter befriended me, charmed my daughter and made us feel welcome. That's his way. Then his world turned upside down when his ex passed away, and he suddenly became the only parent all at once. He loves his boys, has always been a good dad. But a few months ago, he had to grow up and become the responsible one. And it's scared him."

"And then I come along and upset the world he's created for his boys."

"I don't think it's that so much as they're active, always trying something new. As much as he wants to, he can't wrap them up in cotton to keep them safe. A lot of things can happen on a ranch, and that's one of the reasons he's started showing them the ropes of life here. So they can see the dangers, and learn to be safe."

"Then I show them something new and different, and they want to try that."

"You're not to blame. If he'd gotten to be friends with the male stunt double, the boys would have wanted to do the same thing."

Mackenzie's thoughts flashed to her and Hunter that afternoon in bed.

"What are you thinking about? Your face just got redder than an apple." Kelsey held a hand up. "Wait. Something happened between you two, didn't it? Is that why you're so upset?"

She nodded. "I don't know what to do."

"Just give him some time. He'll calm down. Now come on. Nash and I will drop you off at the cabin." Kelsey stood up.

But she still wasn't ready to see Hunter. "There's a library here, isn't there?"

"Yes, at the other end of the lobby."

"I want to drop in and find something to read. Will that be okay?"

"Sure. We'll wait for you."

"I'm no' ready to go back just yet. You go ahead. You need your rest to carry that linebacker around every day," Mackenzie said, pasting a smile on her face.

"Okay, if you're sure. Have the concierge call someone to take you to the cabin when you're ready. I don't want you wandering out there at night."

"Good night. Thanks for the talk."

"Anytime. Night," Kelsey said, and walked out of the dining room.

Mackenzie paid her check, picked up her tea and

walked through the lobby to the door marked Library. She opened it, relieved to see it was empty. She was amazed at the space. Floor-to-ceiling bookshelves lined two of the walls, and a third made of glass looked out on the darkened ranch. A fireplace spanned an adjacent wall. A couple of overstuffed couches and several chairs invited a person to sink down and stay awhile.

Reading over the titles, she found a mystery and took it down. She grabbed a knitted blanket from the back of one sofa and sank down into the cushions. Curling up, she got cozy with the book.

She needed to escape for a while, forget about Hunter, stunt work and life in general. And books had always done that for her.

But she couldn't quite settle into the story, and finally set the book down. The nagging feeling that she needed to just forget about Hunter and everything between them wouldn't let her go.

She needed to keep her head down, concentrate on work. And leave as soon as she could.

Then figure out how to get on with the rest of her life without him and his boys.

Chapter 17

Hunter burst through the lodge doors and headed for his dad's office. His heart beat so fast he thought it would burst from his chest.

"Dad, hit the emergency line, we need all hands."

"What's wrong?" his dad asked. "Calm down."

"Don't tell me to calm down. She's missing!"

"Who is?"

"Mackenzie. She didn't come home last night. She's not at the movie set. No one has seen her."

His dad picked up the phone on his desk.

Bunny walked into the office. "What's going on?"

"We need a search party. Mackenzie is missing. She didn't come home last night," Hunter said, frantic.

Bunny took his hand. "Angus, put the phone down," she said. "Hunter, calm down. Come with me."

She led him out of the office and across the lobby to the library. Putting her finger to her lips, she quietly opened the door.

He peered in the room. Mackenzie lay curled up on the couch, snuggled into a blanket. Relief hit him so hard his head spun. He'd been frantic, thinking something bad had happened to her.

Bunny touched his arm, and he nodded and slipped inside. He heard Bunny close the door behind him.

He walked to the couch and knelt in front of Mackenzie. He almost hated to wake her up. A little crinkle marred her forehead, as if whatever had bothered her the night before still plagued her.

Guilt pricked him when he realized it was him. Had he hurt her so much the night before she hadn't felt she could come home? That she needed a time-out from him?

He laid a hand on her arm, and she jerked awake. Her eyes focused on him, but she didn't say anything.

"You okay?" he asked.

She nodded, still silent.

"I saw this morning you hadn't come back and was worried."

"Are ye goin' to yell at me again?"

"I didn't yell—" He drew a deep breath. "I guess I deserved that. I'm sorry."

"For what?"

"For what what?"

Her forehead crinkled. "What are you sorry about? For last night, or just now?"

"Last night. I wasn't yelling now."

"Then I'm sorry, too."

"Why are you sorry?"

"For disrupting your life, your boys' lives."

"You didn't disrupt—"

She raised a red eyebrow at him.

"Okay. You did disrupt, but in a good way." He brushed a lock of hair off her forehead. "I can't imagine now not meeting you. Getting to know the incredible woman you are."

Her cheeks grew so red he imagined they were scorching her skin.

"So we're friends again?" she asked.

"I'd say more than friends." He leaned forward, touched his lips to hers.

She met his mouth, tentative. He didn't want to scare her away, meant to keep it light. But her lips were addictive, and he wanted more. Cupping her cheeks, he kissed her over and over, showing her how he felt.

Her breath hitched, and he gathered her closer to his body. She wrapped her arms around his neck, pulling him closer to her.

The door behind him opened. "Hunter, you in—oh, sorry." The door slammed.

Hunter eased back from her, frustrated they'd been interrupted, frustrated they weren't somewhere they could take this deeper, but most of all, frustrated that he'd hurt her to begin with after she'd told him she trusted him.

"Who was that?" she asked.

"Kade. I forgot we're helping Nash today."

"Oh."

"He wants to get the nursery set up as a surprise for Kelsey, so all us brothers are going over there to knock it out."

"That's nice of you guys."

He shrugged. "Family."

"Do you need extra help? I don't have to report on set till later today."

"Naw, we got it. But thanks. How about I drop you at the cabin on my way? You can take a nap in a proper bed." He grinned. "Maybe I can join you?"

She smiled, shoved him back. "You've got plans, boyo. And you need to fulfill your obligations."

"Yeah, yeah."

She bit her lip. "Do you want me to watch the boys?" she asked.

He hated to hear the hesitation, knowing it was because of him. "Thanks, but they're already over at Wyatt's with their cousins." He stood up, held his hand out. "Come on, and I'll drop you off at home."

It struck him then that she had very much become a part of his home. And it didn't scare him as much as it should have.

She took his hand and stood, gathered up her bag and they walked out of the library.

Hunter pulled up at Nash and Kelsey's cabin. It had been hard dropping Mackenzie off at his place and not being able to follow her in. But he'd promised to do this ages ago.

Inside the cabin, he heard hammering coming from the back room, so he followed the noise. Nash had given up his smaller cabin and moved into the bigger one Kelsey and her mom had been using. The third bedroom was being turned into a nursery for their baby.

"Yo. I'm here," he said.

"'Bout time," Nash groused.

"I was busy."

"Can you start putting the crib together?"

Hunter walked over to the box with the crib pictured on it.

"Yeah, I saw how *busy* you were," Kade snapped.

"Whoa. What's with you?" Hunter asked Kade.

His brother shrugged. "You know what I'm talking about."

"Yeah, and it's none of your business."

"You're going down, just like the others." Kade turned back to the shelves he was painting white.

"What 'others'? You wanna enlighten us as to what you're bitchin' about?" Nash asked.

"Mackenzie." Kade tossed the name over his shoulder.

"What do you mean, 'going down'?" Wyatt asked, pointing a hammer at Kade.

"You've got to find a way to get over this hatred you have for women, Kade," Hunter said.

Kade turned around, gave him a dirty look. "I don't hate women."

"Well, one woman," Luke said.

"Eh, she deserves it," Kade said.

"You never should have married her," Luke said.

Kade shrugged. "But then I wouldn't have Toby. He's worth the hell she put me through."

"Then let go of this thing you have against us all finding someone," Wyatt said.

"You and Nash were lucky," Kade admitted. "Looks like Hunter might be the next to go down."

"Hey, I'm right here," Hunter said. "Go down where?"

"The aisle." Nash snickered.

His stomach flipped, then flopped. "Who said I'm getting married? I just like Mackenzie. We're nowhere close to a commitment." The paint fumes must have been getting to him, because his head spun.

"You stringing her along?" Nash asked, pointing a paintbrush dripping sage green on the tarp covering the floor at him.

"No," he squeaked. He cleared his throat. "No. We're just—just—seeing what's between us."

"Don't mess around with her. She's not that type of woman," Nash said.

"Jeez. Just because you have a daughter now doesn't mean you have to look out for all the single women everywhere," Hunter said.

"Not my point," Nash said. "She's fragile."

Hunter sputtered. "Fragile my butt. She's strong, fit and brave. She can outride, outshoot and do handsprings around all of us…" He let the words die.

All four of his brothers had turned around and were grinning at him.

"You got it bad, dude," Wyatt said, and they all laughed. "You're totally in love with her. Just don't realize it yet. Don't forget—you're the one who caught the bouquet at my wedding."

Hunter huffed, and spread the pieces out according to the instructions. *Just ignore them. Catching the flowers didn't mean anything. Get this done and leave. So I can sneak away early and see what Mackenzie—*

He paused. Maybe he did have it bad. Picking up the instruction sheet, he tuned the others out and concentrated on the directions. Slowly working through the process, the crib started taking shape.

"…pie."

Hunter whipped his head around. "Pie? Who has pie?"

"I thought that would get your attention," Wyatt said. "We're breaking for lunch."

"No pie?" He pouted.

"I know by now anytime you're involved, there has to be pie. Come on," Wyatt said, slinging an arm around his neck.

They walked into the kitchen, and Hunter's stomach growled. Sandwich platters, bowls of potato salad, coleslaw, and chips and dips were spread out on the counter, along with a cooler of beer. And sure enough, several pies sat on the opposite counter.

"Awesome," he said, and grabbed a plate. "Who set all this up?"

"Bunny and Mrs. Green brought it down from the lodge for us."

"See, Kade? Two more good women," Hunter said, and piled his plate with food. He grabbed a beer and sat at the table. He bit into a roast beef sandwich as one by one his brothers joined him.

"How much longer is the movie crew going to be here?" Nash asked.

Hunter held still, waiting for the answer.

"I talked to the director last night. He said they have a few more days filming outdoor scenes, few more in the empty barn, then they'll finish up in LA," Kade said.

"Any damages?" Wyatt asked.

"None I've seen. But you might want to ride out to their shooting locations and check. I'll email you the list when I get back to the office."

"Is Mackenzie staying the whole time?" Nash asked.

Hunter shrugged. "Not sure. She'd mentioned a while back she wouldn't be needed for the whole shoot, then she'd be off looking for her next job."

"Must be a rough life, not knowing if or when you'll have your next job. Takes a toll on a body, too," Luke said.

"She likes it," Hunter said, though he agreed with Luke.

"You going to ask her to stay?" Nash asked.

Hunter took a big bite of his sandwich, purposely chewed the recommended amount of times, then swallowed and drank a sip of beer. "Why would I?"

"You gonna date her commuter-style? Traveling back and forth will get old," Luke said.

"We haven't gotten that far," he admitted.

"So ask her if she wants to stay on for a while. Once the crew leaves, she can stay at the lodge," Wyatt said.

Hell no, was his gut reaction. IF he asked her to stay on a while, and IF she agreed to it, he'd want her to stay right where she was.

The key word was *IF*.

Chapter 18

Mackenzie brushed Rory till he shone, listening to the Triples as they did their own chores. Which of course involved much shoving, shouting and grumbling. Hunter had stepped out for a business call but promised he'd be right back.

"It's times like these I wish I had me own Bodachan Sabhaill," she said, pitching her voice loud enough over the boys'.

"What's that mean?" Eli asked.

"It's a who, not a what. He's a spirit who haunts barns in Scotland."

"A ghost? In a barn?" Tripp's eyes grew extra wide.

"More a spirit, much like what we call a brownie, a magical being."

"Magical? Nuh-uh," Cody said.

"Oh, yes. I told you before Scotland is an ancient land, so of course there are magical beings all over the country."

"Did you ever see any?" Eli had scooped oats into

a pail, now he held the scoop in midair, oats trickling from it to the wooden floorboards.

"Of course. Many times."

"Are they good magic or bad magic?" Cody pushed the broom closer to her.

"Some good, some not so good. I like the good ones the best, of course," she said.

"What's the barn one? The backen shovel?" Tripp asked.

"Bodachan Sabhaill," she said, pronouncing it slower for them. "Like I said, he's a spirit that haunts barns and farms. And do you want to know what he does?"

"Scares the animals?" Tripp chimed in.

"Nope."

"Spins hay into gold!" Cody said, and threw a handful of hay up in the air.

"That's Rumpelstiltskin, dummy," Tripp said.

"Tripp, is it nice to call your brother names?" she asked mildly.

"Sorry," Tripp mumbled.

"Any other guesses?"

"Tell us!" Eli shouted.

"He does all the chores on farms, and sometimes in the barns," she said.

"Chores?" Cody asked. "That's boring."

She set her hands on her hips and looked at him. "So you *wouldn't* like a spirit to do all your chores for you?"

Cody thought about it, his lips twisting one way, then the other. "Yeah, I guess if it's just a boring spirit, might as well do my chores for me."

She laughed. "Very generous of you."

"Chores are boring," Cody said, twisting the broom back and forth.

"Well, they can be. But if you know the secret to doing them, they can be fun."

"There's a secret to making chores fun?" Tripp asked, a note of *the grown-up is fibbing to get me to do chores* in his voice.

"Take Rory, here," she said, patting the horse's neck. "He's my best friend. We've worked together on many movies. He knows just what to do to keep me safe, and how to do tricks and stunts. So to thank him, I make sure to take good care of him, and that he's clean, and brushed down every time we ride, and that he's fed and happy. So don't you think that's a good thing?"

"Yeah, I guess," Cody said.

"And the other animals. They're all God's creatures, and some need taking care of more than others. I want to do my part to make sure they're safe and sound and happy."

Eli nodded. "That's why you wanted to get the kitty out of the tree, right?"

"Yes, that's right." She knew Hunter had talked to the boys about her stunt job, but she wanted to make sure they understood. She loved these boys so much and never wanted them to get hurt trying something they shouldn't. "And speaking of the kitty, and what I did. Come here for a minute, boys."

She pointed to a hay bale for them to sit on, then sat on the ground in front of them. "Remember when I taught you to do the tumbling?"

"Like Spider-Man!" Cody said.

"Yes. I want to make sure you understand that my job as a stuntwoman can be lots of fun, but it can be dangerous. I had to go to a training camp, and I still go to classes to learn new stunts, and how to do them safely. There's also a stunt boss who makes sure everything is safe. I couldn't just walk onto a movie set and do these things. I don't want you to get hurt trying to copy me, okay?"

The boys nodded half-heartedly, not meeting her eyes.

"Cody? Tripp? Eli? Please, promise me you won't try to do the things I've done. I don't want any of you hurt. How do you think it would make your dad feel if something happened to you?"

"Okay," Tripp mumbled.

"I care about you boys very much," she said. "If you ever have questions about wanting to do something, you ask me, or your dad, or a grown-up. It's for your own safety and well-being," she said, and her voice cracked.

They launched off the hay bale and piled on, hugging the stuffing out of her. And she hugged them right back, as tight as she could.

Saints, she loved these boys.

Footsteps shuffled behind them, and she looked back to see Hunter walking toward them.

"Everything okay?" he asked.

"Right as rain," she said, thickening her accent on purpose, trying to put a happy note in her voice.

"Finish your chores, boys," he said.

The boys piled off her, and Hunter held a hand out to help her up. She took it and stood, but he didn't drop her hand.

He looked behind him at the boys, then back at her.

"I told you I talked to the boys."

No way could she miss the annoyance in his tone. "Yes, but I just wanted to emphasize that it could be dangerous."

"They're my kids. I need to keep them safe."

"I'm sorry. I thought I could help."

"Thanks, but I'll handle it."

She pulled her hand from his and looked at her watch. "I need to get to the set. I'll see you later." Grabbing her bag, she hurried to the location for the day. Worry and anger warred in her stomach. How could Hunter be angry at her for wanting to ensure the boys were safe?

Tom's voice penetrated her thoughts as she approached the set. "I was just about to call you. We've made some changes to the schedule," he said, and handed her several pages.

She glanced at the one on top and almost got sick on the spot. "I didn't think we were doing the fire scene yet."

"Study the script. Walk it through with Brody. We'll be filming it tonight." He walked toward the assistant director.

She stared after him, fear almost choking her.

Someone touched her arm, and she jumped.

"I was wondering where you were," Brody said. "We need to get the fire scene laid out."

She told her feet to move, to follow him, but she had trouble getting them to do it.

He looked back at her. "Are you coming?"

Finally, she followed him into the barn.

He showed her the setup. The heroine was supposed to run to the barn to escape the bad guy, but he would trap her and set the barn on fire. Most of the fire would be special effects, but for the close-up shots of her escaping, it had to be real fire.

Brody had specially lined garments for her to wear to protect her from getting burned, plus she would be holding a thick horse blanket over herself.

She tried to block the memories of being trapped in the fire, which seemed like just last week.

"Mack, are you listening to me?" Brody tapped her arm.

"Sorry. I'm just—"

"Scared," he finished for her.

"Yeah, I am. I've been trying to psych myself up to it, but now that it has to be tonight, I don't know…"

"You have to do this. There's not enough time to get another double out here. It'll halt production. You don't want to be in breach of contract, do you? You can do this, Mackenzie. I have faith that you can handle it. Faith in you. Come here," he said, and pulled her into a bear hug.

Brody was great at his job, and she trusted him when it came to the safety of the stunt doubles he worked with.

The door creaked open, and she looked up to see Hunter walk in.

"Mackenzie, I—" He stopped when he saw her and Brody.

"Hunter, have you met Brody? He's the stunt coordinator. Did you need me?"

"I was just going to tell you to call me when you're done, and I'll give you a ride home."

She ran a hand through her hair. "Thanks. I'm not sure how late I'll be, but I'll call when I can, let you know when I get an idea."

"Okay. I'll let you get back to it." He backed out and the door banged closed.

"Is there something going on with you two?" Brody asked.

"Why?" she asked, knowing her face had to be as red as her hair.

"Because of the way he looked at you."

"I don't know what you're talking about." She turned away, then glanced back at Brody. "How did he look at me?"

"Like he wanted to kiss you, whisk you away somewhere you two could be alone."

She frowned. "No, he didn't."

"You know you can talk to Uncle Brody, right?" He cocked a hip and folded his arms across his broad chest.

"Yes. No. I don't know." She huffed out a breath. "I can't deal with him right now. Show me again what I'm supposed to do." She forced thoughts of Hunter away so she could concentrate.

The next few hours, they walked through the scene several times, and she read the script. Part of her job was to get in the character's head, much as the actors did, to know how to react realistically, to mirror what the actress she doubled for would do.

The fear part was easy—she had that down, no problem. It was the rest of it that scared her to death.

They broke for an early dinner and were to report back at eight for wardrobe and makeup. Most of the crew headed up to the lodge for dinner, but she wanted to be alone, so she walked to Hunter's cabin. By the time she got there, she was shivering. But was it from fear or the cold?

She opened the front door just as Hunter pulled into the driveway. He got out, and let the boys climb out.

"I told you to call me when you were ready," he said, walking toward her. He stopped, looked at her face. "What's wrong? Did something happen?"

She shook her head, looked at the boys and forced a smile.

The boys ran into the cabin, and she followed, hoping to slip off to her room. But Hunter touched her arm. "Talk to me."

"I have to go back tonight and work. They moved the fire scene ahead of schedule. Just need to clear my head."

Hunter stared at her a moment, then pulled his cell phone out and pressed a button. "It's me. Can the boys spend the night with you?" He listened for a moment. "Great. Thanks, dude. They'll be ready."

"You didn't need to do that. I'll be fine. I'm just going to my room."

"Go take a hot bath and relax. I'll get the boys ready to go, and see you in a bit." He pressed a kiss to her cheek.

She walked into her room and shut the door, grateful she'd been stranded and had to move into Hunter's spare room.

It was going to rip her apart when she finished the job and had to leave.

If she couldn't do the work tonight, she'd be leaving sooner than she'd expected. And with a cloud hanging over her name in the movie business. Once it got out she'd failed to perform, she would not be hired again.

She ran a hot bath and stripped out of her clothes while the tub filled. Then she sank in, reveling in the heat. Breathing in and out, she tried to relax and get her mind off work.

Her thoughts drifted to her brothers. It was too late to talk to them now, but she'd call them in the morning.

Once the water had cooled, she drained the tub and dried off, then bundled into her fluffy robe. Rubbing a towel through her damp hair, she walked into the bedroom and stopped short.

Hunter lay on her bed, feet crossed, arms propping his head up.

"Wha' are you doin' in here?"

"Waiting for you."

"Where are the boys?"

"Wyatt already came and got them."

"Seriously, you didn't have to send them off."

"They love campouts with the cousins. I wanted to give you some downtime, peace and quiet."

Guilt pricked at her conscience. He'd done this for her. "That's nice of you, but what must Wyatt and Frankie be thinking?"

He gave her a lascivious grin, wriggled his eyebrows. "What do *you* think they'll think?"

She couldn't help it and she laughed, even though she was mortified.

"Besides, when Wyatt was seeing Frankie, her son learned the joys of cousin campouts and grandparent nights. So they're used to it."

"You have an amazing family. You're very lucky."

"Yeah, I am." He rubbed his hands together. "I made dinner," he said, then got off the bed and went to a cart she hadn't noticed by the door. He wheeled it to the chair by the window and gestured for her to sit.

She pressed a hand to her stomach, swallowed hard. "I don't think I can eat."

He handed her a glass filled with bubbling liquid.

"I definitely can't drink anything with alcohol."

"It's ginger ale. Thought it would settle your stomach."

She took the glass and sat on the chair. "Thanks."

"So you want to tell me what happened?"

"They decided to make some changes to the shooting schedule. I don't know why—and I know better than to ask."

"Can't they get someone else?"

"I can't lose my job. I don't want a black mark on my name in the movie business. Brody will be there, and he'll watch out for me."

"Brody, the stunt coordinator I met earlier?"

"Yes. We've worked together on quite a few films."

"Was he the one on the film where the stunt went wrong?" He rubbed a hand through his hair so it stood up.

She laid a hand on his arm. "No, that was someone else. Brody is good at his job. He's got my back."

"I do, too, you know."

She smiled at him. "Thanks for being there for me." Their conversation in the barn earlier had been nagging at her. She needed to clear the air. "You know I've got your back as well, right? That's why I spoke to the boys earlier about my stunt work."

He waved a hand. "I know. And thank you for caring enough about my kids to caution them."

She blew out a breath, relieved he wasn't angry with her. Raising the glass of ginger ale to her mouth, she noticed her hand shaking.

He took the glass from her and set it down. "After getting to know you, and seeing what you are capable of, you can do this." He picked her hand up and kissed the back of it. "Come on, let's get some dinner into you."

"I really don't think I can eat."

"Just some of this soup, maybe a sandwich. Something light, okay? You need to eat something so you can focus."

She leaned forward and kissed his cheek. "Wha' did I do to deserve you?"

"I don't know, but you must have been a *very* good girl. I'm a catch, you know."

"Yes, you've told me that before." She laughed. "Okay, let's eat." She sat back on the chair, and he pulled another one next to the cart.

He took the cover off bowls of soup and a plate of sandwiches.

"The boys are gone for the night. How about if I go

with you for moral support? Think your director would let me be on the set?"

A warm feeling cascaded through her. "I don't think you could be on set—an insurance thing, I'm sure. Besides, it'll be a late night."

"I'll drive you up there, and ask where I can go that's close enough to cheer you on but that won't interfere with any rules and regulations."

"Thank you," she said, and relaxed enough to eat some soup.

"Anytime, darlin', anytime."

She could get used to this.

Used to him.

Used to the boys.

Used to being part of a family.

Chapter 19

Hunter drove them to the location, and they went looking for the assistant director. They finally tracked him down in the trailer set up with sound and monitors. He said as long as Hunter stayed out of sight and quiet, he could watch from one of the unused monitors in the trailer.

He walked Mackenzie to the wardrobe trailer. With all the spotlights set up, it could have been the middle of the day. Cables and wires ran everywhere, and people scurried around, intent on their jobs.

"I better go now," she said.

"You'll do just fine. I know you can do this. You're a very brave woman, you know?"

She looked up at him. "You think so?"

"Absolutely. Come here." He pulled her into a tight hug, and she squeezed him back. Going on instinct, he moved back enough to give her what he'd intended to be a quick kiss, but turned into a toe-curler for him.

And by the dazed look on her face, he thought she might have some curled toes, too.

He went back into the sound trailer and sat on a stool in the back, out of the way. The monitor was already turned on, and he tuned out the murmurs of people at the other end of the trailer.

Mackenzie walked into view on the monitor, her hand pressed to her stomach as she talked to Brody.

She'd told him they would do several run-throughs first, without the fire. He watched as she got into position and pulled a big blanket over her head and back. She had to run across the barn as if dodging flames and falling beams, which she'd said would be added later, then kick out the side door. The movie crew had built a fake door, so the real one wouldn't be damaged.

After running through it once, including kicking out the fake door, she met with Brody and Tom, the director. Hunter assumed they were giving her notes or feedback. Somewhere in the distance, he heard the trailer door open and close, and footsteps walked up behind him.

"Hunter? What are you doing here?" Carley asked.

"Oh, hi." He briefly looked up at her. "I drove Mackenzie out here." He looked back at the monitor again, trying to determine Mackenzie's body language, gauge how she was doing as they started the run-through a second time.

"You're in love with her."

It took a few seconds for her words to make sense. "What?"

"Mackenzie. You're in love with her."

"No—I—no. Why do you say that?"

"I can just tell. You were never that interested in me during our little flirtation."

"But—I—"

She laid a hand on his shoulder. "It's okay. I was still in love with Bryant."

She glanced at the monitor showing Mackenzie up close. "She's a good person. I have a feeling she'll keep you in line," she said, and smiled, then walked over to speak with the assistant director. A few minutes later she left the trailer.

"Huh." He stared into space. She was the second person to say that he was in love with Mackenzie. Was it true? And if so, was it that obvious? Even to a virtual stranger?

How did he know what being in love was like? He thought he'd been in love with Yvette, but it hadn't been enough to sustain them even a year into the marriage.

He loved his boys, and his family.

Was it love when you wanted to be with someone all the time? To wake up in the morning next to them, be the last person they see at night?

Was it love to want to put their needs first, their happiness?

Movement on the monitor drew his attention, and he watched as Mackenzie ran through the process twice more.

The fourth time she pulled the blanket over her head, someone lit it on fire.

Hunter tensed, and he had to force himself to watch objectively, have faith that she knew what she was doing.

By the time she kicked through the fake wooden door, he was on his feet. She came through the splintered wood, and she was supposed to trip over a piece of wood then fall. But he saw the terrified expression on her face as she shifted the horse blanket just before she fell forward. His heart nearly burst out of his chest, and he panicked that something had gone wrong.

The director called "Cut" as Hunter hurried out of the

trailer. Two crew members were spraying her down with fire extinguishers, and suddenly the flames were out.

But she lay still. Too still.

He slid in the foam and fell to his knees next to her as crew members lifted the horse blanket off her back.

"Mackenzie? Honey?" He rubbed the back of her hand, afraid to touch her if she'd been burned.

Her head lifted, and tears poured from her eyes.

"Where are you hurt?" he whispered.

She squeezed his hand and coughed. She tried to say something, but he couldn't hear her.

"What?"

"I'm fine." She turned over gingerly and sat up. Her face was covered in black smoke, tears still ran from her eyes, but she was smiling, her teeth showing white against the soot. "I did it!"

He heaved a sigh of relief, then coughed on the smoke still drifting in the air. He leaned forward and pulled her into his arms.

She pushed against him. "I'm filthy. Don't want to get you dirty."

"Darlin', clothes will wash. I just want to hold you. You're so brave," he said, and felt like bawling for some reason.

"Mackenzie, you did great," Brody said from above them.

"I did, didn't I?" she asked, and Hunter helped her stand up.

"Yup. Tom said to congratulate you, and you're released for the night."

"Thank God," she muttered, just loud enough for Hunter to hear her.

"Let's go home," he said, and put his arm around her shoulders.

"Sounds good. I'll be right back. Need to change."

He didn't want to let her go even long enough to change, but he had to give her space to absorb what she'd done tonight, the fears she'd overcome.

While he waited for her, he watched crew members scurry around, intent on their jobs. He was used to having guests at the ranch, some of them on work retreats, but having a movie crew was new. And he wasn't sure he really liked it.

"I'm ready to go if you are," Mackenzie said as she walked up to him.

She'd changed into her own clothes and washed off as much grime as possible.

He slung his arm around her shoulders and guided her toward his truck. The farther they walked, the clearer the air became.

He opened the door for her, and she climbed in. She yawned, then slapped a hand over her mouth. "Sorry."

"You're exhausted. I'll get you home right quick."

By the time he'd navigated the quiet roads to his place, she was asleep.

He parked the truck, then quietly opened his door and got out. He walked to her side of the truck, but stopped. Looking up at the night sky, he noticed the stars seemed to shine even more brilliantly than usual. He loved living out here, where he was surrounded by the land he loved. The people he loved.

Her door creaked open. "Are we home?" she asked, yawning.

Her calling his cabin *home* gave him a warm feeling, and it felt right. "Yeah, we're home."

"What were you looking at?" Mackenzie asked, her voice sleepy.

He pointed up. "Just thanking the Almighty for keeping you safe tonight. And looking at the stars."

"Wow. What a gorgeous view. It's a lot like home. I really miss it." Her voice got low, and he heard the note of sadness.

"Think you'll go back soon?"

"Oh. I'd like to. Have to save up enough for a ticket. So maybe between jobs I can."

"I've never been there. Think the boys would like to go?"

"Definitely." She laughed. "I can just see them now, camped out at Loch Ness, spyglasses trained on the water, waiting for Nessie to appear. As determined as they are, they'll probably be the ones to prove she's real."

He chuckled. "Between Nessie, the castles and the ghosts, they'd have a blast." He glanced at her. "Come on, let's get you inside. It's been a long day."

He held her hand while she climbed out of the truck, then put an arm around her waist as they made their way to his front door. He unlocked it and they walked to her room. "Why don't you take a shower and get ready for bed?"

"I'm actually hungry now," she said, her stomach growling.

"I can whip something up for you. What do you want?"

Her stomach growled again, and she blushed. "As hungry as I am, I could go for a full Scottish breakfast."

"What's in that?"

"Eggs, bangers, black pudding, baked beans, mushrooms, broiled tomato—"

He held a hand up. "Baked beans I've had for breakfast before—riding on the trail. But what are bangers and black pudding?"

"Bangers are sausage. Remember the haggis?"

He nodded.

"Black pudding is sort of similar."

He wrinkled his nose. "Okay, stop there." He thought of what he had in the fridge. "How about steak and eggs? A ranch breakfast."

"Brilliant. I'll be out soon."

"Take your time." He watched her go in her room and close the door, then walked to the kitchen.

He found steak in the freezer and set it to defrost, then pulled eggs out of the fridge. Smelling smoke, he checked the stove to see if he'd left it on. Finally realized it was coming from his own clothes. He strode into his bedroom, opting to shuck his clothes and hurry through a fast shower.

As the water pounded down on him, he thought back over the evening, and to what Carley had said.

He waited for a pit to grow or bats to flit around in his stomach. But other than a little ping, he didn't feel scared. He felt right.

But how did *she* feel?

He knew she liked him—now. They hadn't gotten off to a great start, but their relationship had grown.

Should he just wait and see what happened next? "Heck no. I'm going to ask her."

Mackenzie took her time showering, making sure to wash every bit of smoke and grime down the drain. She was exhausted and elated, bone-deep tired and brimming with excitement. Tonight, she'd done what she'd been terrified of doing since the accident.

And she knew she owed a great part of her courage to Hunter. He'd stood by her, encouraged her, didn't push her, just let her decide for herself.

What a man.

Walking out of the bathroom, she debated about getting dressed, then glanced at the clock. Just after midnight. Might as well put on her pajamas and be ready for bed. She pulled on her flannels, fluffy robe and slippers, then walked out to the kitchen.

The scent of meat cooking hit her as she neared the kitchen and she almost swooned, she was so hungry. Hunter stood at the stove, turning a steak over in a pan.

"It smells delish in here," she said.

"Oh, you like? My new aftershave." He patted his cheeks.

"Is it called Eau de Steak?" She laughed. "You goofy man."

He pouted. "And here I got all cleaned up just for you." He struck a pose, holding the cooking fork in the air. He wore the navy blue pajama bottoms with dancing polar bears again and a blue thermal shirt.

She didn't know what it was about a man in a thermal shirt, but she loved the look. Or maybe it was this man in particular.

"Yes, I dressed up for dinner, too, as you can see." She strutted several steps across the kitchen as if she were a model, then pulled the neck of her bathrobe up and posed like it was a mink coat.

He stared at her, an odd look on his face.

"Something wrong? Hunter?" She waved a hand at him.

"Nope. Everything's fine. Fried eggs okay?" He turned back to the stove and set the fork down.

"Fried is great. Can I help?"

He cracked eggs into the skillet. "How are you at toast?"

"Brilliant. Best toast maker in the Highlands." She giggled.

"Did you just giggle?" he asked, turning his head to look at her.

She put a hand over her mouth. "I think I did. I guess I'm happy," she said, and did a cartwheel on the way to the counter to make toast.

"Now who's being goofy?" he asked, and pointed at her.

She walked up to him and pulled his head down, then smacked him on the lips. "Yer eggs are burning."

The surprised look on his face made her laugh, and she picked up the loaf of bread. She put bread in the four-slot toaster, then opened the fridge door to collect butter. A jar of strawberry jam sat next to the tub of butter, so she grabbed that also.

As she closed the door, she noticed three new drawings had been added to it. She studied the first one—a castle rose high, with gray scribbles scattered all around.

"Know what those are?" Hunter asked.

"A castle? Not a clue about the rest, sorry."

"Ghosts. Tripp must have remembered your story about the haunted castle."

She laughed and admired his creativity. The next one hung in the middle. "That's definitely got to be Nessie. And she's wearing my hat!" She leaned closer. "And is that…?"

Hunter walked up next to her and pointed with the spatula. "Yup. Dead farmer."

Cody's name was scrawled across the bottom of that one. "Bloodthirsty little lad, isn't he? Where does he get that from?"

Hunter walked back to the stove, shaking his head. "No idea."

Giggling again, she moved on to look at the last picture. Eli had drawn the lake, mountains and trees, and five people holding hands. Hunter, Eli and his brothers, and a woman with a bunch of curly red hair. Touched beyond belief, she then noticed he'd drawn an angel with yellow hair, looking down at them from the sky. "Is that…?"

Hunter glanced up. "His mom."

"Wow." She swallowed the tears in her throat. For him to include her in the family meant so much to her. "What a beautiful drawing. He's talented."

"He loves drawing."

"Remind me to take a picture of these, if that's okay with you?"

"I'll get copies made for you—they'll love it that you want copies for yourself. They all consider you part of the family."

She smiled, her heart full of love for those little lads.

While he finished up the eggs and steak, she set plates and silverware down on the island. Somehow it seemed cozier to sit there with him, instead of at the big family table.

The toast popped, and she plated it, set it on the island, too. She sat and watched him as he placed eggs and steak onto their plates. The aroma made her mouth water.

She cut into the steak and took a bite. "*Well tidy scran*. This is the best steak I've ever eaten in my life," she said, cutting another piece. She shoved it into her mouth, anxious to taste it again, and noticed him staring at her. "Wha'?"

"You want me to put another steak on the grill for you?"

She laughed and shook her head. "This is plenty for

me." Taking another piece of toast from the plate, she slathered it with strawberry jam, then dipped it into the egg yolk and ate it. Finishing up the steak and eggs, she sat back, finally sated. "Thank you for cooking."

She looked up to see him staring at her. "Do I have something on my face?" She swiped her lips with the napkin, but he didn't say anything.

He leaned toward her, slow-like, keeping his eyes on her. "You're one hell of a woman, Mackenzie Campbell. Where have you been all my life?"

Chapter 20

Hunter's words made Mackenzie's heart sing. No one had ever said anything like that to her before. She was wearing pajamas, no makeup, sitting in the middle of his kitchen, and she felt happy, desirable and more like a woman than she ever had.

"You're pretty incredible yourself, Hunter Sullivan."

She leaned forward, meeting him halfway. Their lips touched, soft kisses that led to more intense kisses. Lips meeting, sliding, testing, tasting.

He got up from the bar stool to pull her up. She went gladly, wanting to laugh with joy as his arms wrapped around her.

"I want you," he whispered in her ear. "Stay with me tonight?"

She nodded, and he led her to his bedroom.

She hadn't been in his room yet. Like her room, the walls were wood paneled, with a wall of windows looking out to the mountains. It was masculine, like he was. Heavy wood furniture, a bed as big as the lake outside, and dark green and navy accents furnished the space.

What a coincidence. Two of her clan tartan colors.

Then she spied a giant squishy chair shaped like a cherry pie sitting in front of the window. Several smaller pillows that looked like cherries were thrown in the middle.

And she started laughing. She laughed so hard she had to clutch her stomach.

"What are you laughing at?"

She pointed at the chair.

"What's wrong with my pie chair? It was a Christmas present from the boys. I'll have you know it's very comfortable. See for yourself." He picked her up and dumped her in the middle of the pie chair.

She sank into cloud-like softness. "I must admit, it is very comfortable—for a pie chair," she said.

He stood over her, hands on hips. "Although there's one thing I've wondered about that chair."

"What's that?"

"If it's big enough for two."

And he turned around and tumbled backward into the chair next to her. His added weight made her side rise up, and she rolled over on top of him.

"Aha! Right where I wanted you, my pretty Scottish miss." And he cupped her cheeks, pulling her head down to meet his lips.

He devastated her with that kiss. His hands roamed over her back, molding her to fit against him.

Sparks followed wherever he touched her, igniting her blood, sending her spinning out of control.

She craved him—his touch, his kisses, his body.

All of him.

Straddling him, she untied her belt, then took her robe off. He watched her, his eyes gleaming in the soft lamplight.

She slid her hands up to the buttons on her pajama top and flicked the first one open.

"Let me," he said, his voice low and husky in that way that made her insides flip. He brushed her hands away and unbuttoned the second button on her tartan plaid flannels.

With each button he opened, his fingers trailed fire down her skin. Then he slid the top off and stared at her.

"Man, you're beautiful."

Liquid heat pooled in her belly even as her face warmed from his blatant admiration.

"Maybe you should take your shirt off so I can see you," she said saucily.

He sat up so fast, she almost fell backward. This time, he didn't play around as he took his thermal off.

"You're pretty beautiful yourself, cowboy," she said, tracing the line of muscles on his chest and stomach.

"Not handsome?"

"Oh, aye, handsome, too. Beautiful. Like a Greek god." She hadn't meant for the words to be spoken, but they'd tumbled from her lips before she could stop them.

He grinned. "Awesome." Then he looked down. "We need to lose the bottoms, don't you think?"

"Why yes indeed. They're covering the best part."

He looked back at her and burst out laughing.

She stood and put her hand out for him, helping him up. But as soon as he was on his feet, he swooped her into his arms and carried her to the bed.

Instead of setting her on the floor, he encouraged her to stand on the bed. He pressed a kiss to her belly and hooked his fingers into her pajama bottoms, sliding them down, taking her panties with them. He kissed her belly again, then shucked his own bottoms.

He wrapped his arms around her and pulled her close, resting his head against her.

She threaded her fingers through his hair. "Is something wrong?"

"No, just savoring this moment." He lifted her to the floor, then kissed her.

She slid her hands down his back, feeling the muscles shift beneath her fingers. She'd never wanted anyone the way she wanted him.

Somehow he maneuvered them to the side of the bed and pulled the covers down. He followed her onto the bed with continuous kisses.

As they made love, she felt a bone-deep connection with him. This was the first time she'd ever felt this way.

Who would have thought she'd have to leave Scotland, move to Los Angeles, then go to Montana to fall in love?

Love? She rolled the word around in her head, realized that yes, indeed, she'd gone and fallen in love with this Montana cowboy. Her heart galloped even faster.

She'd have to proceed with caution. Her mum's words of warning ran through her head, albeit a bit quieter this time.

But still, best to be careful for now.

Hunter woke the next morning under a heavy weight. He glanced down and realized it was Mackenzie, sprawled halfway on top of him.

He grinned. She didn't hold back. She was comfortable being herself.

She was the perfect woman for him.

He glanced at the clock. Ten minutes before his alarm was due to ring. Maybe he could wake her up and they could—

No, he should let her sleep. She'd had a rough day and could use the rest. She'd told him during the night she wasn't needed on set till this afternoon. Besides, they'd woken each other up several times during the night—not that he was complaining.

Their lovemaking had been phenomenal. Earth-shattering. He'd never used words like that before, in bed or out.

He needed to get up now, or he would end up staying in bed with her all day. He tried sliding out, but she was pretty much deadweight on top of him. He rolled slightly toward her, until he could slide her off him. She grunted something, then rolled back onto her stomach.

He hurried through his shower and shaving. With a towel slung around his hips, he walked back into the bedroom. Mackenzie was sitting up in the middle of his bed wearing his thermal shirt. Her red curls were wild, and he decided he liked her hair best that way. Completely natural and free.

He walked to the bed and pressed one knee on it, leaned over and kissed the top of her head. "Morning, sunshine."

"Hmmph," she said, and rubbed a hand over her face. She did not look quite awake yet.

"My shirt definitely looks better on you than me," he said.

She glanced down at herself, as if surprised at what she was wearing. "It was the first thing I came across." Then she looked up at him. "I like that towel on you." She smiled.

He struck a pose. "It's from the Bathroom Collection."

"You should take it off and come back to bed," she said, running a finger along the edge of the towel. Her touch jump-started his libido, and he was tempted to do just that.

He glanced at the clock. "As much as I'd love to get wrapped up in you again, I have to go to work. But why don't you stay here and get a few more hours' sleep?"

The words surprised him, but he found he meant them. He liked seeing her in his bed. And wanted to keep seeing her there.

But he shouldn't want that with the boys at home. He had to be a role model, a responsible dad. She could maybe take some vacation time, live up at the lodge, and they could date. But he'd miss her being in his cabin all the time, laughing with his boys, looking at him with those pretty green eyes.

Then maybe he should think about marrying her.

He blinked.

Marriage?

They'd just met a short time ago.

"Hey, Hunter? Where'd you go?" she asked.

"Huh? What'd you say?"

"I said, I think you need to play hooky this morning and get back in here with me." She tugged on the towel, and it started slipping from his hips.

He backed away. "Tell you what," he said, yanking the towel off. "How about this stays with you?" He flung it at her, then walked to the closet, buck naked.

She wolf-whistled behind him, and he shook his butt a little.

Her laughter followed him all the way into the closet.

And he realized it was just one more thing he wanted to hear every day for the rest of his life.

Chapter 21

Mackenzie worked out, then met with Brody about the last stunt she would do on the film. This one would require her to walk the narrow rafters near the barn's roof. Filmed out of sequence, this would actually lead up to the fire scene they'd shot the night before.

The character was supposed to cross from one hayloft to the other to avoid being caught by the bad guy. She and Brody spent a couple of hours in the barn while she walked the rafters, making sure they were all sturdy enough.

Once they were through rehearsing, Mackenzie hopped down and took the safety line off. It had to be sturdy enough to hold her if she fell, but thin enough to be hidden on film.

Brody climbed down from the hayloft to go meet with the director. She coiled the safety line, checking it for any tears or nicks that could endanger her safety.

She heard something creaking down in the barn and looked over the edge. Nothing she could see.

She decided to get a sandwich at the lodge, and

climbed down the ladder. Once on the ground, she turned around to see Eli crouched next to one of the hay bales. She laid the safety line with the rest of the stunt equipment.

"Hey, sweetie. What are you doing in here? Shouldn't you be in school?" She sat on the bale next to him.

"It's recess. I wanted to see what you're doing."

"I was rehearsing." Had he seen anything?

"I saw you. You're brave to walk up there so high. Were you scared?"

"Well, I've been trained for this, and I was wearing safety equipment. My stunt boss was here to make sure I was okay, too. And you should never try it, remember?"

He looked up at the rafters, then nodded slowly.

"Shouldn't you get back to school?"

"I guess." He kicked at something with his boot.

She put an arm around his shoulders. "What's wrong, lad? You don't look too happy."

He sniffled. "Grampa said you're leaving soon. I don't want you to leave," he cried, and flung his arms around her.

She wrapped her arms around him and pulled him into a hug. "Shh, it's okay. I promise I'll keep in touch."

"No, you won't. You'll go away and we'll never see you again, just like Mommy."

"My love, it's not like that. You know the difference, right? I'm going home to Los Angeles. It's not too far from here. I can come visit you, or maybe you and your dad and brothers could come see me. We could go to Disneyland." She rocked him till he stopped crying.

"You live by Disneyland?" he asked, and hiccupped.

"Yes, and it's a lot of fun."

"Promise we can see you?"

"I'll do everything I can to make sure we stay in touch, and get to see each other."

"Oookay."

She found a pack of tissues in her bag and wiped his eyes, then had him blow his nose. "Now come on, you need to get back to school." She took his hand and walked him to the building where classes for the ranch kids were held in winter.

Her heart broke for Eli. He'd looked so forlorn. She'd have to talk to Hunter, let him know Eli was still struggling with his mother's death.

She'd come so close to promising him she would stay. Deep in her heart, it was what she wanted to do. Montana was a far cry from Hollywood, though, and she worried that if she was out of sight, she'd be out of mind for future jobs on movies. She'd worked hard to get where she was in the difficult world of stunt work.

She'd fallen in love with Hunter and his boys.

Could they make a life together work?

Hunter walked back into his office after a meeting. It had been hard concentrating on the details when all his thoughts were on Mackenzie, and trying to figure out when—and how—he should tell her he was in love with her. Should he talk to his boys first? Make sure they were okay with it?

He grinned, knowing instinctively they'd be fine with having her around all the time.

His cell rang and he saw it was Wyatt calling. He hit the speaker button. "Yo, Wyatt. How the heck are you? How's the family?"

"Get down to the southwest barn right away. Eli's fallen and is unconscious."

Hunter's heart stopped. He hung up and ran out of the office, bumped into his dad.

"What's wrong, son?"

"Eli's hurt!" He kept running out the lodge doors and across the lawn to the barn. The snow had started melting, making it harder to get traction.

A group of people stood outside the barn, and he looked for Wyatt. Just as he reached the door, Mackenzie ran up.

"Someone said Eli's hurt. Where is he?" she cried.

"I don't—"

"In here," Wyatt shouted from inside the barn.

He hurried in, Mackenzie close behind.

Cody and Tripp sat on one of the hay bales, crying.

Eli lay facedown on the wooden slats of the barn floor. Not moving.

A thin rope and a couple of hay bales sat near him.

Oh, God no. Not my baby.

He knelt on the floor. "Has he been out this whole time?"

"Yeah. I was outside fixing the fence. Cody came and got me. I called Nash. He's bringing Kelsey to look at him."

"There's a medic on the crew. I'll get him." Mackenzie squeezed his shoulder, then hurried outside. She was back shortly. "He's on his way."

"I don't understand why he was in here," Hunter said. Eli hadn't moved. He was afraid to touch his son, yet wanted to gather him up and hold him close.

Mackenzie knelt next to him and Eli. "He was in here a few hours ago while I was rehearsing in the rafters—"

A cold spike of fear struck his heart. "You let him watch you?"

"No. I didn't know—"

A red haze clouded his vision, and he couldn't breathe.

"Get out," he snapped.

"Hunter—"

"I said get out. I don't ever want to see you near my sons again. You've done enough. It's okay if you want to keep putting yourself in harm's way doing stunt work. But you can't do it around my boys."

"You don't understand—" she said. Tears poured down her face, but his heart had turned to stone.

"You're not welcome here. Get. Out. Now." He turned his back on her and leaned over Eli, willing him to wake up.

His dad hurried into the barn with Bunny. She went straight to Cody and Tripp and gathered them up, took them outside. They kept saying something, but it was so garbled from their crying Hunter couldn't understand them.

More footsteps pounded the floorboards, and Nash and Kelsey came in. She had a medical bag with her. Nash helped her kneel on the ground, and she grabbed a stethoscope out of her kit. She moved it over Eli's back, then took his pulse. "Steady but weak."

Another man hurried in with a medic bag. "I'm Billy, the crew medic."

"Hunter, move back, let them work on Eli," his dad said.

"No, I have to stay close."

"I understand. We'll just be right here. But they need room to work. Come on, son."

His dad put a hand out, and Hunter grabbed it and stood. They moved back a few feet. Dad put his arm around Hunter's shoulders. He was numb, dead inside. If anything happened to Eli, he'd never forgive himself.

Or Mackenzie. How could she have let Eli watch her rehearse? Especially after they'd discussed it?

Nash and Wyatt stood with them, then Luke rushed into the barn with Kade.

Kelsey beckoned Hunter over.

"We're pretty sure he's got a fracture in his radius, the lower arm. He's still unconscious. We need to get him to the hospital in Billings as soon as possible."

"I already called the hospital, and they're sending the Life Flight helicopter. Should be here soon," Kade said. "I'll clear these people out." He walked out of the barn and cleared the group of people watching, waiting for word on Eli.

Hunter stayed by his son, praying like he never had before.

It felt like hours to him before he heard the chopper blades outside. Three EMTs rushed in with a gurney. Two of them checked Eli, while the third asked Hunter to fill her in.

"He must have been up in the rafters and fell."

"What was he doing up there?"

"A stuntwoman has been here with a movie crew, and we think she let him watch her rehearse."

"Did she let him go up in the rafters?" the EMT asked.

Hunter blinked. "I don't think so—surely she wouldn't do that."

One of the other medics signaled her, and she nodded. "He's ready to go. You're coming, right?" she asked.

He nodded, looked at his dad and brothers. "Can Cody and Tripp stay with one of y'all?"

They all nodded.

"I'm going to have Nash drive me to the hospital," Kelsey said. "We'll be there as soon as possible."

"You don't need to be driving all the way to Billings in your condition," Hunter protested, even as Nash opened his mouth to argue, too.

"I want to be there," Kelsey said, shutting both of them down.

"Where's Maddy?" Hunter asked.

"Frankie has her, Toby and Johnny," Nash said.

As the EMTs wheeled the gurney bearing Eli outside, Hunter's phone rang. He glanced at the readout and saw it was Bunny.

"Bunny, we're just getting on the chopper."

"Something you need to know. Mackenzie's not—" Bunny said.

"I have to go. I'll call you later." He pushed End on the phone and hurried to the helicopter.

The EMTs got Eli boarded and strapped in, then he climbed in next to his son and buckled himself in.

"Can I touch him?" Hunter asked the EMT closest to him.

"Yeah, the connection would be good. He'll know someone he loves is with him."

The door shut and then they were airborne.

He laid his hand on Eli's unhurt arm and didn't let go for the whole trip to Billings.

Once they'd landed, Eli was unloaded from the chopper and wheeled toward the door on the roof. They took the elevator down to the emergency room.

Hunter started to follow the gurney as they wheeled it into a big room. A nurse grabbed his arm.

"I need to go with my son," he said, trying to free his arm from her iron grip.

"Mr. Sullivan, I need some information from you first. We'll be able to help him much faster if you cooperate. Let's sit down over here." She led him to a table and chairs in an alcove.

The secluded area was quieter, and he was able to think a little more clearly.

The nurse started firing off questions and he froze, not sure how to answer. Then he remembered a little card his ex-wife had given him before she died. He pulled it out of his wallet and handed it over. It had all the information he was too rattled to remember.

The door to the waiting room opened, and his dad, Nash and Kelsey walked in. Hunter waved them over.

"How did you get here so fast?"

"I called in a favor from a neighbor," his dad said. "Got a ride on the chopper he uses to monitor his stock, then grabbed a rental car at the airport."

Kelsey hugged Hunter. "Any news?"

He tried to shake his head, but it felt all jerky. He was so grateful they were there.

"Come over here and sit down," Kelsey said. They took up residence on a couch and chairs in the corner. "Bunny and I talked to Cody and Tripp after you left."

"Are they okay? I should have talked to them before we took off, but it was so hectic."

"They know you love them, and that you were worried about Eli. Look, what you think—heck, what we all thought—happened, didn't."

"What?"

"Eli wasn't imitating Mackenzie. He wasn't up in the rafters."

"He wasn't?"

"No. The Triples went to the barn to play and saw the hay bales. They wanted to practice lassoing, so they helped themselves to one of the safety ropes the crew left in the barn. One of the ropes got stuck on a beam, so the boys stacked up two hay bales to try to get it down. That's how Eli fell."

Kelsey told him she'd already given the information to the ER staff, so they'd be aware the fall wasn't as high as they'd feared.

He tried to process it, but his worry about Eli consumed his thoughts.

"Mr. Sullivan, Eli is awake," the doctor said as he walked up to their group.

"How is he?" Hunter asked, tears clogging his eyes.

"His radius is fractured, he has a mild concussion, but otherwise he's a lucky boy. We'll keep him overnight for observation. But you can see him now."

Hunter wiped his eyes and followed the doctor into a small room. Eli lay on the bed, his arm in a cast. He was pale, but he was alive. Hunter hurried over to the bed and kissed Eli's face over and over.

"Daddy, stop it," Eli said, laughing weakly.

"Do you know how worried I've been? How worried we've all been?"

His son looked down. "I'm sorry, Daddy. We were playing and Miss Mack's rope got caught. I didn't want her mad at me for taking it."

"Eli, she wouldn't have gotten mad at you."

But she must hate *him* after the horrible things he'd said.

"Is she here?" Eli asked, looking hopeful.

"No, I think she's at the ranch."

"I don't want her to leave," Eli said, tears gathering in his eyes.

"I know, son. I know."

"She said she would come visit, but that's not the same."

"When did she say that?"

"Today."

"What else did she say?"

"That she's not going away like Mommy did."

Hunter's heart stuttered.

"And she said we could go visit her, and go to Disneyland!" Eli said. "But, Daddy, if she came to live with us, can we still go to Disneyland?"

Hunter laughed, and he relaxed. "Would you like that?"

"Yes! We all wanna go to Disneyland."

"No, I mean for Mackenzie to come live with us at the ranch."

"In our cabin?"

"You boys love her, right?"

Eli nodded, moving his head carefully.

"I'm pretty sure I love her, too. What if she and I were to get married?"

A smile broke out so wide on Eli's face Hunter worried he might break his cheeks. "Yay!" he shouted.

"Shh, better keep it down, son."

"Okay, Daddy." Eli yawned. "Daddy, I'm tired."

He kissed his son's forehead. "You sleep. I'll be here."

He bowed his head and took a minute to give thanks for Eli being fine, for the EMTs and ER staff, for Kelsey and for his family.

And to pray that Mackenzie would forgive him.

Chapter 22

During the long night in the hospital, Hunter tried Mackenzie's cell phone a dozen times, but it kept going to voice mail.

Frustrated and anxious to talk to her, to apologize, he finally called Frankie around six in the morning and asked her to go to his cabin and find her.

Thirty minutes later, Frankie called him back. "She's gone. She packed up and left. I tracked down Brody, the stunt coordinator, and he said she told them she couldn't do the last stunt and quit. She hired one of the ranch hands to drive her to the airport last night. Brody said she couldn't get a flight out till this morning. Her Delta flight leaves in forty-five minutes to LA."

Hunter's heart sank. He'd done this. Caused her to quit and run off.

"Did you hear me?" Frankie asked.

"What?"

"I said move your butt, she's at the Billings airport."

Billings airport.

He was in Billings.

"Thanks, Frankie. I owe you big-time."

He ran down the hall to Eli's room and opened the door. He was awake, and Nash and Kelsey were sitting with him.

"Eli, you okay if I go out for a little while?"

"Where?"

"To get Mackenzie."

"Yes, Daddy!"

Nash pulled a set of keys out of his pocket and tossed them to him. "Rental's in the parking garage. P2. Go."

Hunter ran out of the hospital, then to the parking lot, beeping the key fob until he finally heard the right car. He got in and drove as fast as he could down the two levels, all but threw money at the parking attendant, then hightailed it out of the garage.

At least traffic was light, and he made it to the airport in record time. He parked as close to the terminal as he could, then dashed inside. Spying the Delta desk, he ran to it and cut in front of a person slowly approaching the counter.

"Someone is getting ready to board the flight to LA. It's urgent I reach her before the plane takes off."

"The flight to LA?" The counter person looked at her screen. "I'm sorry, sir. That flight took off early and is airborne now."

His world caved around him.

He was too late.

Mackenzie picked her backpack up. She needed to find a shop in the small airport that sold cell phone chargers. She'd left hers at Hunter's cabin, and her phone had died shortly after getting on the road to Billings. All the Sullivan numbers were on her phone, which was dead

dead dead. She'd called the hospital, but they wouldn't give any information out to someone who wasn't family.

She stood up and stretched, aching after sitting in the airport all night. Walking toward the row of shops, she decided to get a cup of tea.

She unzipped her backpack to get her wallet out, and bumped into someone. "Oh, excuse me—" she said, and looked up.

"Mackenzie? Mackenzie!" Hunter yanked her into his arms, squishing the backpack between them.

"What are you doing here?" she asked, shock and happiness warring for a spot in her brain.

"*Me?* What are *you* doing here? Your plane just took off."

"I couldn't get on not knowing how Eli was." She burst into tears. She fumbled in her coat pocket. "Oh, where's a bloody tissue when you need one."

He pulled several napkins from a nearby container and handed them to her. They sat down at a small table by the window.

"How is he?" she asked, wiping her face and blowing her nose.

"He's fine. A fractured arm, mild concussion. They kept him overnight, but we can take him home today."

A fresh round of tears cascaded down her face, and she sobbed. "I'm s-s-so happy."

"I need to apologize to you. I blamed you thinking Eli was copying you, trying to do your stunt in the rafters."

"He wasn't?" She sniffled, confused. She'd seen the rope lying near him.

"Cody and Tripp told Kelsey they were using your rope to practice their lassoing. It got caught, and Eli climbed up on the hay bales to try to get it down."

She closed her eyes, guilt flooding her so fast her

head spun, and she had to lay it down on the table. She'd been sick with grief ever since the accident. She shouldn't have left the safety equipment in the barn for any length of time. Should have put it away.

"Will you forgive me?"

"For what?" she asked, not moving.

"For being so ugly to you yesterday."

She raised her head, then sat up slowly so the room wouldn't spin again. "You were worried about your son. I understand. I shouldn't have left anything behind in the barn while I went to eat. Can you forgive me?"

"I think we need to forgive each other. I'm really sorry. I shouldn't have lashed out at you."

Could she believe him? Should she? He'd gutted her with his words the day before. They weren't hers, but in the short time she'd been at the ranch, she'd fallen hard for the triplets. And for Hunter. "You can trust me—I'd never do anything to hurt your boys."

"I was terrified. He was so still, not moving. I thought I'd lost him. But I shouldn't have hurt you." He turned his hand over, palm up, on the table. "Will you come back with me?" he asked.

She stared at his hand, not sure what he meant. What he wanted from her. "To the hospital?"

"Yes, and to the ranch."

She hesitated. "Why?" She laid her hand on the table, next to his, a fraction away from his. But afraid to take that last step and trust him.

"For one thing, you can do the stunt you missed last night. Finish the job. Keep your good reputation."

"Wha' are you sayin'?"

"The boys love you."

"I love them." A little kernel of hope unfurled in her chest.

"And I love you," he said, and closed his hand over hers.

"You do?"

"Yeah." He kissed the back of her hand. "So…what do you think?"

She smiled. "Well, I suppose I love you, too."

The grin on his face grew and grew and grew.

And then she saw it.

The love he felt for her was written on his face.

And she knew. They were meant to be.

"Me and the boys will pack up and move to LA, wherever you need to be to keep working. Think they have—"

"Hunter—"

"—good schools there? Be a big—"

"You don't need to—"

"—change for us, but we'll get used to it. How big is your apart—"

She cupped his cheeks. "Would ye stop talking, you bampot?"

"I guess you could go on without us, so you can find your next stunt job. We can look for a house. Need something big for all of us."

She laughed. "Well, you could go to LA, but I'll be here in Montana."

"That's what we'll do. You fly to LA, we'll have to get a moving van out anyway. Maybe I can get Kade or Luke to drive my truck…" He stopped talking and looked her in the eyes. "Wait. What? Why would you be here?"

"I'd much rather live here. I told you once it reminds me of home, right? The land, the wide-open spaces, your family… I love it here."

"But your job."

"Maybe I can find something to do on the ranch, take an occasional stunt job."

"You'd really be happy here?"

"Yes. I never liked living in LA. Too crowded. This place, your family—I love it here."

"Think you could marry a rancher from Montana with triplet sons?"

"Oh, aye. I think that would be the grandest adventure in the world."

He stood and pulled her up and into his arms. Framing her face with his hands, he kissed her. She sank into his lips, knowing without a doubt this was where she belonged.

Chapter 23

One month later, and the whole family was sitting down in the lodge dining room for the rehearsal dinner. Hunter checked his watch for the hundredth time. Where the hell was his surprise?

Everything had gone great the last few weeks. Eli was home safe and sound. The director had rehired Mackenzie, and she'd completed the last stunt and fulfilled her contract. The movie crew was gone, and a semblance of normalcy had returned.

Until Bunny gathered the women and they went into a frenetic wedding planning mode. Which wasn't all that bad. He and Mackenzie had opted not to wait too long to get married. The ceremony was tomorrow, and the honeymoon would be in LA, to pack up her apartment and move her to the ranch for good. They'd agreed she would travel from Montana to wherever her jobs took her, and he and the boys would join her when they could.

But now Hunter was worried his plans for his gift to Mackenzie had fallen apart.

The waitstaff started bringing out plates and serving

everyone dinner. As much as he loved to eat, he didn't think he could swallow a bite.

"What's wrong, love?" Mackenzie asked him, leaning close.

"Nothing. Just hungry." He patted his stomach and she rolled her eyes.

The door to the dining room banged open. "Who here means to take our sister away from her family and her homeland?" boomed a deep voice with a thick Scottish accent.

Hunter looked up to see four men with hair the color of Mackenzie's walk in. *It's about damn time.* He blew out a relieved breath.

"Oh!" cried Mackenzie. She scooted her chair out and ran full tilt across the dining room, holding her flowered skirt up, her red hair streaming behind her.

If Hunter hadn't been watching, he never would have believed it, but she launched herself in the air, landing in her brothers' arms. She kissed their faces over and over, crying and laughing all at once.

They set her down, and she gathered them all into a group hug.

Hunter got up to join them. When she turned to look at him, the happiness on her face damn near poleaxed him.

"Did you do this?" she asked, sniffling back tears.

"I figured they should be here—" He didn't even finish the sentence before she flung herself at him, and he got the same treatment her brothers did.

"Come meet me brothers," she said. "Hunter, that's Fergus with the messy beard, the oldest of the four, then Ian comes next, and Scotty and Graham are the twins. Boys, this is my Hunter." She beamed at all of them as if she expected them to be the best of friends now.

Her brothers all faced him as one unit, legs apart,

arms crossed, thunder on their faces. Hunter started wondering if maybe it hadn't been such a good idea to fly them from Scotland to Montana for the wedding. They hadn't spoken on the phone but the one time, and then he'd emailed them the details. Up close, he realized they were all just a bit taller than him, and much brawnier.

"You," Fergus said, pointing a beefy finger at him. "You dare ta think ye can make our sister happy?"

Hunter swallowed hard, nodded. "I aim to."

"Ha'e ye made her cry?" Ian asked.

"Uh…" He looked behind him at his own brothers. "Guys? A little support here?"

His brothers all stood up and walked toward the group, his dad following close behind.

Mackenzie eyed her brothers. "What're you lot up to?"

"Ne'er mind, sissy. We'll handle this," Fergus said, his eyes narrowing even more.

The Campbell brothers all took a big step forward, crowding Hunter back a few feet. He once again looked back at his brothers. "Well?"

Nash folded his arms, nodded at the Campbell men. "We'll see. Depends on how you answer their questions."

"So, *lad*, ha'e ye made our sister cry?" Ian asked again.

Should he lie, or tell the truth? Which would get him less of a pounding? "Only a little. And I didn't mean to."

The Campbell brothers all stepped forward again, flexing fists, heaving muscles.

A bead of sweat ran down Hunter's forehead. Great—no backup. He threw a dirty look at his brothers, who all grinned at him.

"You boys can pound me into the ground, break every bone in my body and feed me to Nessie. But it won't keep me from loving Mackenzie, taking care of her and wanting to be with her the rest of my life."

All four redheaded men grew even more stern, more forbidding. Then the one she'd called Scotty started laughing, and before long, everyone in the room was laughing.

Except him. *What the hell?*

Fergus stepped forward, hand outstretched. "We're jus' messin' wi' ye, lad."

Hunter clasped Fergus's hand, then as he started to pull it back, Fergus gripped it tighter, to the point of pain, and leaned forward. "But make no mistake. You hurt her, e'er, and we end ye. Got it?" Then he backed away, all smiles again.

Hunter shook hands with each of the brothers, each one saying something to the same effect, low enough for only him to hear.

Mackenzie beckoned the triplets forward. "Cody, Tripp, Eli, these are my brothers. Lads, these handsome boys will be my sons." Her voice broke on the last word, and she dashed a tear away.

"Whoa, now we got eight uncles!" Eli said.

"Oh, great. I guess that means I have eight brothers now," Mackenzie said. Hunter glanced at her, and even though the words were dry, she was beaming.

"It looks like ours is no' the only family wi' multiples," Fergus said. "Yer family will be growing by leaps and bounds."

Hunter swallowed, hard, choked on his saliva and coughed. Ian, who stood closest to him, pounded him on the back.

"Here, drink some water." Mackenzie handed him a glass.

He sipped, finally able to breathe again. "You never told me you had a set of twins for brothers," he whispered.

She shrugged. "I never thought about it." She faced him. "Is that a problem?"

"We haven't talked about having children of our own," he said, his head slowly spinning. He glanced behind him and saw the door to the butler's pantry. He took her hand and pulled her inside, turned the light on and shut the door for some privacy.

"Do ye want more?" she asked, her voice so quiet he had to stoop to hear her.

"I hadn't ever considered it. There was no one in my life to consider it with."

Her face grew even paler than normal, and she pressed a hand to her stomach.

"I also never thought I'd find the love of my life," he said, wrapping his arms around her. "What about you? Do you want children of your own?"

She leaned back, meeting his gaze. "Those boys already are my own. I couldn't love them more if I'd given birth to them myself. But do *you* want more?"

"In all honesty?" Her body tensed in his, and he pulled her closer so her head rested on his shoulder. "I can just see a little girl with wild red curls, running around the corral, learning how to rope hay bales and jump onto a moving horse while she shoots a bow and arrow. I just hope she gets my love of pie."

She burst out laughing, and leaned back, punched his arm. Then she cupped his cheeks and pulled his head down to smack his lips with a quick kiss. "I love you, Mr. Sullivan."

"I love you, 'almost Mrs. Sullivan.'" He leaned forward and captured her mouth in a hot searing kiss. He cupped her butt and pulled her flush against him.

The door flew open. "There you are," Bunny said. She reached in and snatched hold of his ear, then pulled until he let go of Mackenzie and followed Bunny. "There'll be no tomfoolery in my brand-new butler's pantry, young man. You have to wait for the honeymoon tomorrow night."

"Yes, ma'am," he said, and grinned at his bride-to-be.

The next evening, their wedding reception at the lodge was in full swing, and people milled everywhere. The light winked on Hunter's shiny new wedding ring as he lowered his hand.

Mackenzie looked beautiful. She'd decided on a simple cream wedding dress, no fancy frou-frous or lacey bits to clutter it up. Her brothers had brought her the Campbell clan tartan to wear diagonal over her dress like a sash.

Maddy had been in heaven, getting to play flower girl again. This was the fourth wedding she'd been in since Kelsey had moved her little family here. He'd bet anything that she'd already started planning her own wedding.

Kade walked over to stand beside him. "I can't believe you let her talk you into a kilt."

"Why not? Mackenzie's brothers wore kilts today." Even he had to agree that when her brothers all walked her down the aisle, it had been a sight to see. All that red curly hair on the whole bunch, matching kilts and macho muscles surrounding the love of his life.

"Yeah, and on them it looks right. On you? Different story."

Hunter stuck a leg out, examined the dark knee socks and cowboy boots he wore. "You're just jealous 'cause I've got great legs."

Kade sputtered his beer. "Hardly. Your knees are knobby."

Hunter leaned forward and raised the blue, green and black plaid kilt enough to see his knees. "No they're not."

"What are you morons doing?" Nash asked.

"I say his knees are knobby," Kade said.

Nash moved his head to the side and looked down.

Hunter stuck his leg out. "See? Normal knees."

Nash frowned. "Hmm. They look kinda girlie."

"What's goin' on?" Wyatt asked as he and Luke joined them.

Nash grabbed the kilt and lifted it up. "We think his knees are funny-looking. What do y'all think?"

Hunter shoved Nash's hand away. "Hey, watch it. Don't mess with the goods, dude. I don't want to flash anyone."

Nash yanked his hand back. "What're you wearing under that thing?"

"Fergus explained that Scotsmen go commando under kilts."

His four brothers all took a step back, like choreographed dancers.

He spread his legs apart, bent his knees slightly and shook his butt. "It's very freeing, actually. You should try it."

It took everything he had not to bust a gut laughing at the horror on his brothers' faces as they scrambled back away from him even farther. One by one they peeled off in different directions.

"What're you up to, husband?" Mackenzie asked, sliding her arms around him from behind.

"I told them I'd gone Scottish, and I'm not wearing any drawers under my kilt."

"Oh, I like that." She slid one hand down his hip to the back of his leg, and she began pulling the kilt up.

It tickled his thigh, and he grabbed her hand, pulled her around in front of him. "What're you doing, lady?"

"Perhaps I don' want to be a lady right now," she said, a wicked expression on her face.

He held her hand and rubbed his finger against her wedding ring. "In the first place, much as I hate it, we're in public. Second, your brothers are here, and they would bury me if they knew what I was thinking right now."

"Oh? And what's that?" she asked, stepping closer to him.

"Something about the butler's pantry, kilts, free access and making you my wife in all ways until we're both too exhausted to walk."

Her breath hitched, and she pulled his head down to kiss him very thoroughly. He was about ready to make good on the butler pantry idea when someone yanked on his tux jacket.

"Now, now, now," Bunny said. "There's time for that later."

Mackenzie gave an exaggerated pout, and Hunter bent down to her ear. "I've got briefs on—I wasn't sure if Fergus was yanking my chain or not."

"Oh, no. It's traditional for men not to wear anything under kilts."

"Huh. Go figure." He kissed her cheek. "Then when it's just you and me, I'll wear it the traditional way."

She smiled, and started to say something, but Bunny grabbed her hand.

"Come on, Mackenzie. Ready to throw the bouquet?" Bunny said. "Now remember what I told you?"

"About the tradition?" his new wife asked as they started walking away.

Bunny nodded, and they both turned back to look at him.

Tradition? What tradition? There hadn't been any family traditions when his dad got married, or Nash—

The bouquet.

Hunter looked around the banquet room, spotted Nash and Wyatt standing with their wives by the cake table.

He strode over to the group and walked up behind his brothers, draped his arms on their shoulders and stuck his head between theirs. "We gotta see how she does it."

Wyatt looked at him. "Who does what?"

"Bunny. She's got Mackenzie ready to throw the flowers."

"So?" Nash asked, and lifted his bottle of beer. His hand froze midair, and he turned his head to look at Wyatt, then Hunter. "Oh, yeah." He grinned. "This'll be good. Wonder who it'll be?"

The DJ called all the single girls forward to the dance floor as Mackenzie walked in front of them.

"Where do all these single girls come from anyway?" Hunter muttered.

"It's a wedding, bro. Brings 'em out in droves. Neither rain, nor sleet, nor dark of night can keep a single girl from a wedding," Nash said.

"Hey, watch it, pal," Kelsey said, and punched his arm.

Nash grinned then leaned sideways and kissed her.

Hunter grinned. Kelsey was the best thing that had happened to Nash. Wyatt had fallen hard for Frankie, and was a much happier man now.

And himself? He had snagged the love of his life. He faced the stage, just as Mackenzie held the flowers up high. She turned her head around to view the waiting women. "Ready?" She faced the DJ again, and everyone counted.

"One. Two. Three."

She tossed the flowers backward. He, Nash and Wyatt all craned their heads to follow the trajectory as it sailed over the crowd of single women and straight at Kade and Luke.

Kade glanced up. His eyes widened. He dove to the side as fast as a calf avoiding a lasso.

The flowers hit Luke square in the face, showering rose petals all around him. His hands came up reflexively and caught the bouquet as it fell.

Luke stared at the bouquet, several expressions flitting across his face. He finally looked up and realized everyone was staring at him. Raising the bouquet, he used it to salute Mackenzie and Bunny, then his brothers, and walked to the bar and got a beer, clutching the bouquet under his arm.

"So, should we start a pool?" Nash asked.

"When's the next group coming to the ranch?" Kade asked. "I'll take two weeks in."

Nash started laughing. "That romance authors retreat that Bunny booked is up next. They had to postpone it, but they'll be here in the next few weeks."

"Aw, man, that's killer," Wyatt said, and laughed.

Mackenzie joined them, and Hunter put his arm around her, pulled her close.

"Did I do it right with the bouquet?"

"You did it just right, Miss Mackenzie."

The cake had been cut, the first dance danced, the flowers flung.

It was time for them to leave.

Time to start the grandest adventure of their lives.

* * * * *

SPECIAL EXCERPT FROM

HARLEQUIN®

SPECIAL EDITION

*When Shania Stewart tells Deputy Daniel Tallchief that
he needs to lighten up with his wild younger sister,
the handsome lawman doesn't know whether to
ignore her or kiss her. But Shania knows.
It's going to take a carefully crafted lesson plan
to tutor this cowboy in love.*

Read on for a sneak preview of
The Lawman's Romance Lesson,
the next great book in USA TODAY *bestselling author
Marie Ferrarella's Forever, Texas miniseries.*

Shania flushed as she raised her eyes toward Daniel. "I don't usually babble like this."

Daniel found the pink hue that had suddenly risen to her cheeks rather sweet. The next second, he realized that he was staring. Daniel forced himself to look away. "I hadn't noticed."

"Yes, you had," Shania contradicted. "But I think that it's very nice of you to pretend that you hadn't." When she heard Daniel laugh softly to himself, she asked him, "What's so funny?" before she could think to stop herself.

"I'm not accustomed to hearing the word *nice* used to describe me," he admitted.

Didn't the man have any close friends? Someone to bolster him up when he was down on himself? "You're kidding."

The lopsided smile answered her before he did. "Something else I'm not known for."

She pretended that he was a student and she did a quick assessment of the man before her. "You know you're being very hard on yourself."

"Not hard," he contradicted. "Just honest."

She had no intention of letting this slide. If he had been one of her students, she would have done what she could to raise his spirits—or maybe it was his self-esteem that needed help.

"Well, I think you're nice—and you do have a sense of humor."

"If you say so," Daniel replied, not about to dispute the matter. He had a feeling that arguing with Shania would be pointless. "But just so you know, I'm not about to chuck my career and become a stand-up comedian."

She grinned at his words. "See, I told you that you had a sense of humor," she declared happily.

Don't miss
The Lawman's Romance Lesson *by Marie Ferrarella,*
available April 2019 wherever
Harlequin® Special Edition books and ebooks are sold.

www.Harlequin.com